THE CAT BURGLARS

THE CAT BURGLARS

A
FIRST NOVEL

by

Maxine Newman

The Malvern Publishing Company Limited

PUBLISHED BY

Malvern Publishing Company Limited
P.O. Box 16
Malvern
Worcestershire
WR14 1UH
England

ISBN 0-947993-25-8

Printed in Great Britain by
Richard Clay (The Chaucer Press) Ltd,
Bungay, Suffolk

PROLOGUE
MAY 1945

They sat dejectedly around the table, watching the woman crying.

Her dark hair framed a perfect oval face, and was dressed in that unflattering wartime style which made a woman look as if she had a string of sausages wound around her head. Even in the extremity of grief, and despite her unprepossing clothing, she generated an aura of elegance and grace bestowed only upon those of classic bone structure and well-proportioned flesh. Her enormous violet eyes were swollen and discoloured, and she shook uncontrollably.

Women always suffer most, Sam thought. They bring men into this Godforsaken world, calm their first vociferous fears. They watch the fumbles through the early years, teach and guide, laugh and cry. Then along comes another bloody war, and men cheerfully go off waving their stupid flags, singing their stupid songs, and get themselves killed.

With a small gesture of his head, Sam summoned the other two to follow him. They walked softly through the minute kitchen into the equally minute back garden, where a few straggly plants bore mute witness to Nature's determination to survive anything and everything, including the efforts of Hitler's Luftwaffe to obliterate London.

They picked their way gingerly through the broken glass, bits of bricks and general debris which were the legacy of a direct hit on the house next door. Looking at the empty space where No. 26 had once stood, Sam felt a familiar pang of loss for Theda, who had lived there. Named for the famous film vamp of the twenties, Theda had been beautiful, demanding, not always faithful, and Sam had loved her with passionate devotion.

The three entered the old Anderson bomb shelter, and its comforting dark warmth enveloped them. This was where they plotted and schemed, dreamed their dreams, and for the past few years had listened to the world's brave young men passing overhead on their way to slaughter each other.

'Tonight we all stay with her,' Sam pronounced gravely. 'She has taken it very badly.'

'But Sam, Minnie's going to give birth any time, and I promised to be with her.' Butler's tone was petulant, as it always was when he was likely to be prevented from doing what he wanted.

'Sam's right.' Cosie spoke in his usual matter-of-fact way. 'Minnie has managed perfectly well before, and it won't make a bit of difference whether you are there or not. Jess needs us all tonight, so stop being selfish, and remember how good she has been to us. It hasn't been easy keeping us all fed and looked after.'

'I suppose you are right,' Butler sighed grudgingly. 'But at least let me nip over and explain to Minnie. I'll only be five minutes.'

The indifferent moon watched impassively as Sam and Cosie trooped back to the house, and Butler went to make his excuses to Minnie. The moon did not even register these three scraps on the ravaged surface of the earth; the moon would not bother - they were so insignificant. Sam, Butler and Cosie were cats.

CHAPTER ONE
JESS

Jessica Ford was the only child of an impecunious and slightly dotty Sussex vicar. His wife had died giving birth to Jess, and as widowers and their daughters often are, they were very close.

In the way of the English, his parishioners adored their eccentric shepherd, who had been urging them to righteous paths for years, and who had become as dear and familiar to them as the architecture of the old Norman church around which their well-ordered and relatively sin-free village life revolved.

At a fairly early stage of her life, Jess realised that her efforts to be a perfect vicar's daughter were somewhat hampered by the nature of her character, which comprised two distinct and contradictory components. Part of her longed to find joy and fulfulment in the traditional obligations of female inhabitants of vicarages all over

England. She visited sick parishioners, looked after appalling children, listened to endless gossip without repeating any of it, and generally tried to be a paragon of virtue. The other, larger part of her dreamed of escape to an exciting world of glamour and freedom.

She read copiously, most of her choices being frowned upon by Mr. Phelps the local Librarian, a colourless little man whose idea of evil and riotous living was two glasses of parsnip wine in one week instead of his usual one.

'I am not altogether certain that the subject matter of those books is suitable for young ladies Jessica,' he would intone, fussily adjusting his spectacles, as Jess devoured biographies of the great courtesans of the past. Perhaps something a little less prurient would be more appropriate.'

'I'm sure I shall remain uncorrupted, Mr. Phelps,' Jess replied laughing. 'Had she lived in our village, I'm sure that even Nell Gwynne would have led a virtuous life!'

Jess would take her books into the beautiful Sussex countryside, and become for a while Mata Hari, Lillie Langtry, the Empress Josephine. Happy in her own company, being something of a natural loner, she spent as much time in her fantasy world as she spent being the vicar's daughter.

Her great love for her father, and his total inability to look after himself, kept her firmly anchored to the Vicarage, and she was sensible enough to keep her dream world firmly in its place. Just dreams.

Only her friend, the ancient Miss Hortensia La Verge, knew the secret side of Jess, and understood her longing for the greener grass of less restricted pastures.

Miss La Verge was in her late sixties, an unbowed, slender figure, who clung to the elegance of a world which had died with most of its sons by 1918. She lived in a rambling, comfortable old house on the outskirts of the village, with Clarence, an extremely elderly, extremely fat Pekinese, who wheezed and puffed his way through life, and who adored Hortensia as much as she adored him.

Hortensia sat on no village committees, took no part in village life, and didn't give a damn what people thought or said about her. She had been 'on the stage,' in the glittering London of the 1890's, and village gossip insisted that her youth had been sullied by dreadful scandal - even that Royalty had been involved.

In fact, Hortensia had led a very chequered life. On one occasion a minor member of the Royal Family had indeed been the recipient of her favours. His generosity, together with the largesse of one or two other titled lovers, had been her route out of the theatre - 'I was a truly dreadful actress, my dear, but quite pretty.' - and into independence.

In contrast with Jess's hitherto prosaic life, Hortensia had been everywhere and done everything. She had chained herself to railings and finally spent some years married to an American gangster, who went to meet his maker via the electric chair in Sing Sing prison.

'After that little lot, dear, I decided it would be nice to come home and be a quiet old outcast until my end of the egg-timer runs out. I went back to being Miss La Verge. Couldn't bear to be Mrs. Accione after poor Eddie went.'

Jess loved Hortensia, and spent many spellbound hours listening to her reminiscences.

'If only I could live the way you have,' Jess sighed one sunlit afternoon when they were taking tea in Hortensia's garden, during which she had been entertained with breathtaking accounts of the doings of Lucky Luciano, Bugsy Siegal and their various hangers-on and accomplices.

'I know how hard it is for you, my dear,' the old adventuress replied sadly. 'The strongest ropes are made of love. But you are so very young. Who can tell what strange paths you will walk before you become an old lady like me, pottering in your garden and doting on a soppy old dog like Clarence here.'

Clarence underlined how doted upon he was by staggering over to them and helping himself to a large cream bun.

Jess's life went on its uneventful way until her twentieth birthday; in September 1939.

She and her father listened to Mr. Chamberlain's grave announcement, then like everyone else in the island fortress threw themselves whole-heartedly into the business of helping to win the war. The Vicarage's ornate wrought iron gates were donated to make guns and planes, its flower beds and lawn converted to a vegetable garden. Jess sewed blackout curtains and dug for victory, and her father prayed harder than ever before.

At first, their sleepy Sussex village was affected very little by the conflict. Shortages had not yet begun to bite, and the only tangible evidence of a country at war was the squadrons of the Royal Air Force passing over the patchwork quilt countryside of England, the disappearance of the young men into the various branches of the Services, and the sepulchral voices of the BBC announcers, who had little good news to impart to the populace.

Later, Churchill's fighting speeches awoke feelings the British never acknowledge until some catastrophe occurs, and they become truly a United Kingdom. Along with millions of others, Jess felt sure she would indeed fight on the beaches and in the streets if necessary, and would never surrender.

'He understands us you know, old Winnie,' Jess's father observed after they had listened to one of the old war-horse's particularly inspiring speeches. 'He knows that really we British are the most warlike tribe on earth. It's only when we have someone else to fight that we all pull together. If there is no-one else available, then we fight amongst ourselves, and get into the most awful mess.'

The peaceful eccliastic developed a most unvicarlike interest in the strategic conduct of the war. He spread out a vast map of the world in his study, and listened to and read everything concerning the progress of the warriors. As the British Expeditionary Force retreated across France, he marked each fallen town with a Swastika, and muttered and tutted at the incompetence of the Generals.

'Just like the last lot,' he moaned. 'No dash! No imagination! Where are the Wellingtons, the Marlboroughs? What they should have done was... '

Finally the Army was at Dunkirk, with nowhere dry left to go. This ancient nation of mariners sent everything that would float, and many things that wouldn't, to pluck thousands of its sons back home. Had the owl and the pussycat been at home, someone would undoubtedly have borrowed their pea-green boat.

The Hurricanes and Spitfires flew backwards and forwards, their exhausted pilots desperately trying to check the overwhelmingly superior numbers of the Luftwaffe and give some sort of cover to the surrounded troops on the beaches.

The country held its breath, and followed the disaster on the BBC.

Jess was listening to the news at Hortensia's house one stormy May evening, when they heard an aircraft overhead - an aircraft in trouble. They rushed into the garden, involuntarily ducking their heads as the stricken Spitfire passed over, its engine spluttering and coughing and a stream of oily smoke trailing behind. It was losing height rapidly, and seemed almost to embrace the trees as it lumbered towards the village. Finally, gravity was the victor and it crashed somewhere nearby, with a great eruption of smoke and flame.'Oh my God! The Vicarage!' Jess was already running home, followed by Hortensia, who had the totally irrelevant thought that the last time she ran anywhere was when Eddie had given her the keys to his safe-deposit box and shoo-ed her out of the house minutes before the arrival of the FBI, and Clarence, who was trying desperately to remember how to run at all.

The Vicarage was wiped out. The crashing Spitfire had ploughed into its mellow old bricks before exploding, and plane and building had melded into a blazing mass of collapsed masonry and tortured, twisted metal. It was obvious no-one could have survived inside. Jess knew her father had intended to spend the day poring over his map, and stood in shocked silence as the village fire-brigade fought a valiant, but losing battle with the inferno.

When at last the fire had burned itself out, they had to sift through the wreckage to find enough of her father to bury. They interred what was left of him next to what was left of the Spitfire pilot. The Church sent someone to officiate at the funeral, and he droned on about the Will of God. Jess was numb, but felt it was the will of a very strange God to take so kind and gentle a servant in such a brutal way.

In the days following the funeral, everyone in the village rallied round to give what comfort they could. Jess was told of many unsung kindnesses performed over the years by her unassuming parent, and the grief of his parishioners intensified her own feelings of loss. For many days she felt unable to imagine her life without him.

Jess moved in with Hortensia. It was a very simple operation - she had lost everything but the clothes she stood up in.

Hortensia was wise enough to allow Jess time to grieve, and simply fed her and put her to bed, and waited for the natural resilience of youth to heal the wounds.

One day, when she perceived a glimmer of Jess's usual bright self, Hortensia took her up to the loft to rumage in her trunks of old, but splendid clothes.

'You simply cannot go around looking like a rag-bag. It is so bad for the morale. Try this one, I always had such good times when I was wearing it.'

'Really, Hortensia! Where would I wear a fabulous creation like this,' Jess laughed, pirouetting in a shimmering black beaded and feathered dress from the twenties.

'I suppose you are right,' Hortensia conceded. 'So sad though. I would have loved to think of that dress being worn again to wonderful parties. I was wearing it the night I met dear Eddie. At least we can make use of the plainer things. We can alter a few skirts and jackets, and that pale mauve suit will look wonderful on you. It came from Paris you know. So charming Mr. Worth was to me. I bought many of my things from him in my heyday.'

Jess was clever with a needle, and soon had an adequate, if limited, wardrobe to replace her losses in the fire.

'So now we have you clothed, and you have to stand on your own two feet, it's time you gave some thought to what you are going to do with your life. I absolutely refuse to let you fester away her until the world has passed you by.'

They were enjoying a pre-dinner sherry, and Clarence was wheezily dozing at Hortensia's feet. The tranquility of the evening made it impossible to imagine the desperate battles being fought so few miles from where they sat.

'I propose to go to London,' Jess replied. 'I don't know what I shall find there, or what I shall do. But I shall never find out if I don't go and try. Something will turn up.'

'I agree absolutely,' her friend said seriously. 'One should always try. However, may I invite you to spend a little more time with me before you leave? I think you should ease away gently from being the vicar's daughter, and your company would give a boring old lady a great deal of pleasure.'

'Hortensia, you are the least boring person in the world, and the kindest. I should love to stay with you.'

Jess stayed for two months. She then made her tearful farewells, promises to write, and like thousands before her and thousands after, she took the train to London to seek the pot of gold at the end of her personal rainbow.

Hortensia insisted that she accept a gift of £25.

'Just to get you settled dear,' she said, pressing the money into Jess's hand. 'I could not bear the thought of your having no emergency fund. London can be very hard.'

'All you need is a spotted handkerchief and a cat,' Jess thought as she arrived at Victoria station one windswept morning in September 1940. She found the YWCA, and was shown to a cheerless, functional little room. The contrast with the chintzy comfort of Hortensia's house was depressing, and she had to fight the urge to rush back to Victoria and take the first train back to Sussex.

It was obvious that the ability to organise Jumble Sales and officiate at Vicarage Sports Days were not qualifications in great demand in the blacked-out wartime city, and Jess applied for a job as a 'Nippy' - a waitress in Lyons Corner House. She suspected that her success at the interview was largely due to the fact that the Manager thought she would look well in the uniform, and could appreciate a pair of shapely legs as much as the next man, despite the fact that his poor eyesight had dashed his military ambitions.

The work was hard, and the hours long. In the early days, all she could do was droop her weary way back to her room and fall into an exhausted sleep, praying no air-raid warning would drag her to the nearby Underground station which served as a bomb shelter for the local inhabitants.

As she adjusted to the demands of her new life, she explored, and tried to imagine the glamour and excitement of the great city in peacetime - all its lights ablaze, and roisterous crowds thronging its streets. London in wartime had little glamour, and the excitement consisted of racing into a shelter before the bombs began to fall.

Jess felt she was the loneliest person in the loneliest place in the world, and wrote long letters to Hortensia pouring out her misery.

That first Christmas in London was the worst time of her life. She was requested to work, in order that married waitresses might spend the festive season with their families, so the respite of even a brief reunion with Hortensia was denied her.

Christmas in the Vicarage had been a joyous affair, and she longed many times for life to be the way it used to be, forgetting how dull it had seemed at the time.

1941 began with little relief for beleagured Britain. The country held on by the skin of its collective teeth, and prayed for a miracle.

Jess's life gradually became fuller, with invitations from her servicemen customers to dinner or the theatre. As the parks bloomed with daffodils, she realised she was enjoying her independence, and awoke each morning with a feeling of anticipation rather than dread.

After one particularly exhausting day, Jess had been asleep for only a few minutes when the air-raid warning sounded. She groped her way into some clothes, and fled headlong for the Underground station.

In this dank, foetid place, where a yard of space was guarded as fiercely as a week's meat ration, Jess met Richard. Or rather Richard fell over her.

She had wrapped herself in her coat, propped herself up against a wall, and ignoring the crying of children and the conversation of her fellow-shelterers, had fallen into an uneasy doze. She was awakened by someone tripping over her legs. When her tired eyes forced themselves open, she focused on a tall figure in Army uniform retrieving his cap from somewhere between her ankles.

'I'm so sorry,' the figure said. 'I'm recovering from a little disagreement with what seemed like an entire Panzer Division, and the co-ordination's not what it was. Seem to be falling over all sorts of things lately, but I must say you're the prettiest so far.'

'Oh it's all right, just please let me go to sleep. I'm so tired.' Jess turned over and was instantly asleep.

When the general stirrings of the shelter's inhabitants awakened her next morning, she was surprised to find the officer with the co-ordination problem sitting beside her regarding her thoughtfully.

With eyes like those he should be in the Navy, Jess thought. She had read in novels descriptions of deep-water eyes meant to scan far horizons. Now she knew what the phrase meant. His hair was blond, and she thought vaguely, too long to please the Army.

'I couldn't sleep, so I spent the night watching you, and plotting how I could spend some time with you. I do hope you don't mind,' he said with a disarming smile.

'No, I don't mind,' Jess grinned, appreciating his casual charm. 'What did you decide?'

'I decided to invite you to lunch. A good meal will do you the world of good. You are a little thin.'

'I-I'm not the sort of girl who goes out with strangers,' Jess stammered, the Vicar's daughter taking over from the excitement seeker.

'Ah, but these are fearful times, my dear. While we are finding a mutual acquaintance to introduce us respectably we could both be killed. What a waste! To prevent such a catastrophe, I shall do the introductions myself. Richard Grafton, late of Surrey, currently assisting His Majesty's Brigade of Guards to win the war. At your service, madam.'

'Jessica Ford, late of Sussex, currently helping Lyons feed the masses. Pleased to meet you.'

'Pleased to meet you too. Now we've got all that nonsense out of the way, where shall I pick you up, and at what time?'

'As it happens, it's my day off, so I shall be delighted to lunch with you.' Jess flashed her best coquettish smile, as demonstrated by Hortensia. 'As I live at the YWCA, I think it would be better if we met somewhere.'

'Undoubtedly. I love assignations. Let's make it under the clock at Waterloo Station. It's so romantic; everyone meets there. Say 12 o'clock Jess, and we shall have a perfectly splendid afternoon.' He touched his cap, and as he turned to leave, Jess saw he limped very badly, and relied heavily on the support of a walking stick.

Jess rushed back to her room, torn between nervousness and excitement. She spent hours deciding which of the items in her limited wardrobe she would wear to meet this engaging stranger, finally deciding upon Hortensia's pale mauve suit, and a plain white Victorian-style blouse. On her way to Waterloo, she bought a bunch of violets which the street-vendor pinned to her lapel. The cheery little blooms matched her mood, and she approached the rendezvous in high spirits, taking care to be just a trifle late.

Richard was waiting for her at that most popular of meeting places, and informed her she was about to enjoy the best lunch available in London.

They took a taxi to a small Restaurant near the Thames, and were ushered into the back room. The proprietor obviously knew Richard well, and fussed over them outrageously. This particular eating house appeared to be untouched by rationing - at least in the back room - and Richard confided that the proprietor's father was a farmer in 'darkest Essex", and that a fellow-officer was a member of the family. This haven of gastronomy was one of the better kept secrets of the war.

They talked easily that first afternoon. On some subjects their opinions were diametrically opposed, but their disagreements were good-natured, and they laughed a lot. They loved the same music, and had read the same books. The afternoon passed all too quickly for Jess.

It was the happiest day of Jess's life, and she knew there could be no other man for her but the tall, injured officer who helped her into a taxi when they left the Restaurant.

To seal her happiness, as they parted outside the YWCA, Richard kissed her full on the lips, and declared that before their meeting, he had never believed in love at first sight.

They spent every minute they could together. No matter if it was a meal in 'their' restaurant, a concert, a film, or just sitting in a pub, they knew they had found in each other all they ever wanted.

Within a week they were lovers, within a month Jess had left Lyons and they moved into a small house Richard rented in Chelsea.

CHAPTER TWO
RICHARD

Richard Grafton was born to a devoted 'upper-middle class' couple during that time in England's history when for the children of the fortunate few, the summers were always warm, the winter meant roasting chestnuts around a blazing fire, building snowmen, and making a wish while Cook allowed one to stir the Christmas pudding.

The big house in Surrey was always full of life and laughter, and the mews cottage in London was a base for the excursions along theThames, visits to the Tower, and all the excitment available to a small boy in a great city.

He remembered his father Walter as a bluff, kindly man, who always made time for his young son's triumphs and small disasters. His mother, Beatrice, was small and dainty, a pretty little woman, forever entertaining friends, or on her way to Hunt Balls and parties.

Richard was educated at the finest schools, but like most boys, attached more importance to sporting excellence than to academic achievements. Fortunately, he was blessed with an almost photographic memory, and was able to sail through examinations without the grinding slog of study which was the lot of most of his contempories.

The Wall Street crash hit them like a bomb aimed directly at the foundations of their pleasant lives. Walter Grafton loved America with its thrusting, aggressive ways, and played the Wall Street market with skill and enjoyment for years. In nineteen twenty-nine, along with countless others, he was wiped out.

Both the London and Surrey houses had to be sold, together with the motorcars, and treasures which had been in the Grafton family for generations. They moved into a modest rented house in Putney, and for the first time in her life, Beatrice had to cook and clean. There was no money for servants. A Trust Fund established by his grandfather enabled Richard to complete his education, the only relief in the general gloom.

Walter, unable to cope with such radical change in circumstances, took the gentleman's exit route, and shot himself. Beatrice sought refuge in the gin bottle, seeking comfort she never found in the muzzy half-world of alcohol, and viewing the world in which she was a stranger through the bottoms of many glasses. Her pathetic figure at school Parents,' Days had saddened Richard beyond belief. Within two years, she followed her adored husband to the grave; there was just enough money to bury her.

From the age of sixteen, Richard was subjected to the taunts of 'Poor Boy' from his peers at school. His major lesson learned from those years was that poor equalled problems, rejection and ridicule, and rich equalled acceptance, happiness and belonging.

It was the same when he joined the Army. Sandhurst was a constant struggle to make ends meet. Later, in the Guards, Mess bills and gambling debts seemed to breed. He was never out of debt. Always just a bad poker hand away from ruin, he developed a devil may care attitude and quick wit which made him a sought-after companion of his fellow officers, and a magnet to women. At parties, he was the centre of attention; at Galas and Hunt Balls, the County ladies fell over themselves to catch his eye.

Once or twice, Richard considered the possibility of marrying one of the equine daughters of the landed gentry, and living happily ever after on her money. However, his memories of his parents' love for each other always held him back, and he continued to live high on his luck, his charm, and his wits.

Unfortunately, the gods are fickle, and when Richard was twenty-three, his luck turned. The cards would not run for him, and his creditors all seemed to want payment at the same time. He was politely informed by his superiors that it was frightfully bad form to leave one's Mess bill unpaid for so long, and his rich, accommodating best friend and unofficial banker was posted to some forgotten outpost of the Empire to practise his shooting on a few rebellious tribesmen.

It was this disastrous combination of circumstances which led to Richard's decision to become a thief. A very selective and careful thief.

A lieutenant in Richard's regiment invited him to a party at his family's large house in Highgate. During the course of the festivities, Richard familiarised himself with the layout of the house, and planned his raid. He was delighted to note that the family appeared to be stunningly careless with their valuables, they did not keep a dog, and that there was no alarm system.

Richard's second, univited, visit two weeks later, followed a Gala Ball at the Savoy which both he and the lieutant's family attented, held appropriately in aid of Servicemen fallen on hard times. It had been a glittering affair, and everyone had dug out the family jewels.

Richard drank sparingly, but noted approvingly that the amount of champagne being consumed by his intended benefactors would ensure the soundness of their sleep that night.

An Army course in undercover work had obligingly taught Richard the rudimants of breaking and entering, and his natural economy of movement enabled him to glide through the family's bedrooms undetected.

The lady of the house had, by the way of a gift, left a very fine diamond ring on her bedside cabinet, and in a locked drawer in the dressing table, he found a diamond bracelet and a diamond and sapphire necklace, packed in their velvet-lined cases, and ready to leave. Her husband chipped in a pair of heavy gold cuff-links together with a wallet containing one hundred and twenty five pounds. Their daughter, not wishing to be left out, contributed a fetching pearl choker with diamond clasp, and a pair of pearl and diamond earings.

'How generous they are,' thought Richard gratefully, departing as silently as he had arrived. 'And how splendid for me.'

His only remaining problem was to find a fence. How does a hitherto honest man find the means to dispose of his ill-gotten gains?

He had heard that one or two NCO's were engaged in the business of diverting various items of Army property from its intended destination, and probably would be only too willing to point him in the the right direction. One could not, however, just breeze up to a sergeant and ask whom one should contact to dispose of stolen jewellery.

He decided to be a little more devious.

Near to the barracks was a pub of some notoriety. It was strictly an 'other ranks' pub, and officers who ventured in were quickly left in no doubt that their presence was unwelcome.

Richard decided that a little melodrama would be in order. With part of the cash proceeds of his first foray, he purchased a shabby second-hand workman's suit, cap, shirt and shoes. He tinted his hair black, and using scraps cut from his newly raven locks, stuck on a thin moustache. Eyebrows and eyelashes darkened with a woman's mascara set completed his disguise. When he had finished, he posed in front of a mirror in the cheap hotel room he had rented, and defied even his own batman to recognise him.

He made his way to the pub, remembering to slouch along in a most unsoldierly manner.

'The Cat and Fiddle' was a typical soldiers' pub. Representatives of various regiments moaned about the idiocy of officers in general, and their own in particular; asserted that their cooks were the worst in the entire history of the British Army, and discussed the merits or otherwise of various football and cricket teams. They got drunk together, fought each other over causes totally incomprehensible to outsiders, and were finally carted off together by hulking Military Policemen.

Soldiers' pubs never changed. You could get drunk, get a woman, get a fight, get a bet on - anything to fill in time between the action. They were there in one form or another for the soliers of Alexander, or Hadrian, of Napoleon, of Haig. Undoubtedly they would be there when the very last shots were being fired.

Richard shuffled into this strange place an hour before closing time and ordered a pint. The lack of interest he evinced gave him confidence in his disguise. He seated himself on the end of the bench in earshot of several tables, and settled down to tune in on the conversation of interest.

'...the biggest pair of Bristol's you've ever seen! Couldn't believe it mate...'

'...I was that pissed I'd have spit in the General's eye...'

'...so I said I paid for the real blonde, and now I know it's just a bottle...'

'...well that was a goal you'll not see the likes of in a month of Sundays...'

'...but you know you can trust Syd. He don't short-change you for nothing. Always the top rate whatever the gear. Remember when we took him that load of blankets? Could have had us cold. No, I ain't about to change to nobody else. He's done right by me, and I'll do right by him.'

Richard cautiously inspected a corporal and two privates he recognised from his own regiment. He vaguely remembered a comment about missing blankets from the Quartermaster, and now here was the mystery solved. They apparently had been channelled through the trustworthy Syd to grace beds other than those of His Majesty's footsloggers.

'Right so that's agreed. We'll stick with Syd for the shirts and boots. I'll go down to Peckham with them on Friday. Here's to honest Syd Dover, the soldiers,' friend.'

They laughingly raised their glasses, and so unobtrusively did Richard. Honest Syd might not have the resources to deal with stolen jewellery, but he probably would know someone who did.

A battle was about to erupt between two groups from different regiments to settle the question of the relative importance of their forebears' contributions to an obscure skirmish in the Crimea.

Richard finished his pint quickly, and walked to the nearest telephone box. He looked up S. Dover in the telephone directory, and there he was: Number Seven, Church Road, Peckham. Just occassionally the gods will smile on the endeavours of a resourceful man.

CHAPTER THREE
SYD

As outlying areas of London go, Church Road, Peckham was fairly typical. Several snotty-nosed kids played hopsctoch, and an abandoned car was being demolished by a local gifted amateur. Mums chatted to each other outside front doors left ajar to hear possible summonses from the latest off-spring, and a mangy dog nosed around a dustbin.

Richard had chosen to wear an old sports jacket and slacks, and warranted only mild curiousity from the mums, a glance from the kids, and total indifference from the dog.

Number Severn turned out to be second-hand furniture shop, every inch of which appeared to be occupied by bits and pieces. There were big bits - wardrobes, tables and chairs - and bits as small as vases and knives and forks. A tinkly bell sounded as he opened the door, and almost immediately a vigourous figure emerged from a curtained-off back room.

Richard had visualised a seedy, unsavoury character, and was unprepared for the stocky, compact man with a rosy, open face, who introduced himself as the proprietor. Although he generated no air of menace, one sensed that his man could take care of himself, and that behind the genial face was a very sharp brain.

'And what can I find for you today, sir? As you can see, I can satisfy all your needs from soup to nuts, as they say.'

Richard decided that frankness was the only approach to adopt with this good-humoured bender of the law.

'Is there somewhere we can talk privately,' he asked, surprised at the nervous sound of his voice.

Syd looked long and hard at Richard, who felt he now knew how a worm felt, under the scrutiny of a particularly choosey bird.

'You'd better come into the back room. I'll close the shop for a bit.'

Richard felt that in a few short minutes, Syd had sized him up to his own satisfaction or otherwise, and that there was absolutely no point in pussy-footing around the subject of fencing the stolen jewellery.

They were in a cosy sitting room which in no way resembled the cluttered shop. Comfortable armchairs were gathered around an open fireplace, pictures covered the walls, and a marvellous assortment of knick-knacks decorated most of the available surface space. Syd was obviously a man of taste.

'I won't beat about the bush, Syd. I think it best that we are straight with each other right from the beginning. I have nothing to prove that I am not trying to trap you; no references from people you know. I found you by eavesdropping on a conversation in a pub. I'm putting myself in your hands. You can pick up that telephone and I'll go to prison for a very long time.'

'Well then, you had better tell me what it's all about.' Syd had picked up a perfect little porcelain shepherdess, and was flicking non-existent specks of dust from her skirt.

'I have some jewellery to dispose of, and it's a bit on the warm side. This is the first time I've done this sort of thing, and I don't mind telling, confessing that I have absolutely no idea of how one goes about fencing stolen jewellery. Can you help me?'

Syd walked over to the dresser and poured two scotches. Handing one to Richard, he regarded him thoughtfully.

'Seems like I can say I don't know what you are talking about and throw you out, I could call in the law as you said, or we can talk. You get a bit of a nose for people in this game, and I can't smell anything funny coming off you, so we'll talk. I do like money, and times are very hard. I'd just hate to turn you away if there's a few bob to be had. Let's have a look at the sparklers, and we'll see.'

Syd was ecstatic about the jewellery, and they soon worked out a very fair agreement for these, the first delivery, and for any subsequent windfalls which might come Richard's way.

Richard felt completely at home with Syd, and they talked of many things during that first meeting. For the first time, Richard found himself confiding the story of his life.

'There's all sorts of ways people get into thieving,' Syd mused over their fourth scotch. 'For most people, it's sheer necessity. You get your died-in-the-wool villain, of course, and they're hard cases. Like to hurt people. Never get mixed up with them myself, and I'd advise you to steer clear too. Your average thief though, it's usually just 'cos he can't meet his needs any other way. They can be little needs like feeding the wife and kids, or big needs like yours. You like the fast, good life, and sure as hell you won't finance it inspecting squads of soldiers. One thing, though, and remember this carefully, always cover your tracks, and don't trust anybody - except me, of course!'

As Richard weaved a glowing and unsteady path through the shop on his way out, Syd grasped his arm.

'You said you found me by overhearing a conversation in a pub. I need to know what bloody idiot is going around advertising. Next is I'll have the rozzers coming here with nasty questions and search warrants.'

'My dear Syd, I hate to turn informer, but you are absolutely right. You are far too valuable to lose. I would hate to have to find someone else. Besides, I doubt that the decor in Wormwood Scrubbs would appeal to you. They would never let you have your pictures on the wall for start. You can expect a visit from a certain Corporal Bateman with some shirts and boots. He'll be here on Friday. He did praise your trustworthiness to the skies, and it's him we have to thank for what will be a very profitable association. Don't be too hard on him.'

A profitable association it did indeed prove to be.

Richard publicly attributed his new affluence to an unexpected and large legacy from a former admirer of his mother.

Syd was soon able to leave Peckham for the more congenial environs of Brighton, and a nice Regency house, where he indulged his prediliction for pictures and bits and pieces to his heart's content. He had moved up in the hierarchy of fencing, and corporals and Army footwear were a thing of the past. He handled only the proceeds of the best robberies now, and maintained his reputation for fair dealing amongst his limited clientele.

Richard remained his friend and favourite, and all through nineteen thirty-six, nineteen thirty-seven and nineteen thirty-eight, they prospered greatly.

Richard made a point of leaving considerable time lapses between his social visits, during which he planned his burglaries, and his profitable nocturnal returns. If the risks were too high, he would leave the valuables in the possession of their rightful owners. Under Syd's tuition, he learned the arts and crafts of his trade, and took to safe-cracking and alarm busting easily. They diversified from jewellery to pictures, silver, and one favourite occasion, a superb Aubusson rug. Life was good for both of them.

Hitler was an unimportant and disregarded factor in their successful and prosperous lives, and they greeted Mr Chamberlain's return from Munich with glee. Richard considered the war-talk in the Mess to be so much sabre-rattling, and carried on his two professions with success in both fields.

The outbreak of war came as a personal affront. The following months were a blur of Army transports, fighting, and being shot at, being shelled. Killing, losing friends, doing anything to stay alive. Death in all its terrible forms - from fire, from guns, from bombs. Lousy food, sore feet, letters to the families of his men, starting always 'I am sorry ...'. And always, stay alive, keep your head down, stay alive.

Richard would never forget the particular hell of Dunkirk. Having waded exhausted from the beach to one of the little ships loaded to danger point with sodden heaps of the British Army, the slow limp back to England was a nightmare of unimaginable proportions. He was wedged in a minute space next to a sergeant with most of his leg shot away, and crawled off the boat soaked with the man's blood. The sergeant was not so lucky. He would never crawl anywhere again. He would never do anything again.

After Dunkirk, he spent a brief leave with Syd in Brighton.

Syd smoothly transferred his activities to the Black Market. There was no demand for jewellery or fine paintings. Food was the thing, and Syd was in everything from contraband pigs and chickens, to cauliflowers and cabbages.

'Well,' he reasoned to Richard, 'someone's going to do it, so it might as well be me as the next bloke. Thank Christ the Army doesn't want me, and I am doing my bit as the Air Raid Warden.'

Syd enjoyed the power bestowed upon him with this official duty, and took great delight in ensuring that no lights showed on his particular patch to show the Luftwaffe that they were over the South Coast.

'You know I worry about you Richard,' Syd observed one evening as they were demolishing a bottle of illicit scotch. 'There are a couple of medal ribbons on your jacket, and I don't like it at all. I hope you're not getting a touch of the heroics. You should be concentrating on just getting through this lot so we can start up again after the war. Villains are getting killed the same as everyone else. Charlie Preston got blown up last month. One of the nicest blokes I ever met, and the best safe-cracker in England. You just take care of yourself. Get a nice desk job, or shoot yourself in the foot or something.'

'Syd, I have no divine right to survive. No more than the next chap, and a hell of a lot less than most. I can't just order my men to go and get killed, then cower in a shell-hole. Anyway, our lot would probably shoot me if I did. I'll just take my chance - I always have.'

In the event, it was not necessary for Richard to shoot himself in the foot. The reprieve came courtesy of the German Army in Greece.

A particularly adept grenade thrower had decimated a group of British soldiers as they passed cautioulsy through one of the craggy little Greek villages. Richard was one of five survivors, but pieces of grenade and masonry had peppered his legs, severing veins and nerves, and lodging deep in his flesh. He had lost a lot of blood, and the Army doctor had pumped him full of pain-killers. He remembered virtually nothing of the hospital ship which brought him back to England, or the transfer to the grim ward of the hospital.As soon as the doctors would let him leave hospital, he went to Syd's until he was more or less mobile.The Army assigned him a desk job in Whitehall, and within a few weeks of returning to London, he met Jess.

CHAPTER FOUR
SAM, BUTTY AND COSIE

I made a good choice when I picked Jess. She is a lovely lady. I knew she would be the moment I saw her. Old Charlie told me what to look for when you choose your person, and they don't come any smarter than Old Charlie.

Something must have happened to my Mum. I don't really remember much about her. I know she was black, like me, and she was warm and cuddly. I just somehow came to be all on my own, right from when I was a little tiddler. Yes, all on my own I was - until I met Old Charlie, and he took me under his wing, or rather under his paw. Old Charlie was the nearest I had to a Dad. Great big tabby he was; undisputed King of the Streets. Taught me everything I know about surviving when times are hard.

'I know every good dustbin for miles, and I'm going to show them all to you, son. Then we'll go down to the market and snatch a bite from the butcher or the fishmonger.'

We got a nice string of sausages that day, and took them down to the park for a picnic. When we had eaten our fill, Old Charlie sat back and gave himself a good wash. It was getting hard for him to be thorough because of his rheumatism, so I did his back for him.

'Why are you looking after me like this Charlie,' I asked when we were settling down for a nap.

'It's like this, son. I don't like to see a young 'un like you out on his own. Unless somebody looks after you a bit and shows you the ropes, chances are you won't live to be a cat at all, let alone an old cat. We only have nine lives you know, and mustn't use up too many while we're still kittens. Besides, I've no sons left now, what with bombs killing some of them, some moving away, and my two eldest living soft with old Mrs. Hardly in the sweet shop. I want someone to carry on after I've gone. This is a good patch, and I think you're smart enough to run it. No need to live rough, mind. Get yourself a person, and move in. I lived for years with the Blackstock family. Lovely people they were, and it was real comfortable. My own armchair I had, and everything laid on. Would have been there still except for Hitler and his mob. Blew up the bloody house they did. Poor Maisie and Bert got buried, and by the time they was dug out, it was too late. So, I was back on the streets. Nobody wants and old cat, see. You have to get in when you are young and appealing. I never let myself get soft when I had people, though. Good job I didn't! You can find yourself some people son. That's the thing. They can be a nuisance sometimes, but they get to be family.

Not many cats get to keep their own family. Brothers and sisters get sent to different homes, and we lose touch. Every cat should have a family, even if it's only people. You have to choose carefully, though. A woman is best, you are more likely to get spoiled then. Pick one who is quite young, then she's not likely to die before you do, and look for a nice, kind face, and a soft voice.'

'You're enough family for me, Charlie,' I said. 'Cats are better than people, so why bother?'

'Take the word of an old campaigner, son. It's the best way to live. Just say something happened to me. You'd be all on your own, and it gets horribly lonely with no-one to care about, and no-one to care about you. Besides, there's nothing wrong with a bit of comfort. Being stretched out in front of a nice warm fire beats huddling under a hedge on cold nights, and if you play your cards right, you have your person eating out of your paw in no time.'

I was with Charlie for about two months all told. Finest cat I ever met. Never did a dishonourable thing in his life. I doubt I would have made it on my own. He was father, teacher and playmate to me - all in one.

One day we were out mousing on the bomb site, and Charlie cut his paw on some old, rusty wire. Just a little cut it was, and we thought nothing of it at the time. It just would not heal, though, and got all messy and smelly. I settled him in a sheltered place and brought him food, but he just kept getting weaker.

'Come on, Charlie! Get this down you and get some strength back.' I would say when I had found some delicacy for him. 'You can't leave me on my own. You've just got to get better!'

He would pick a little bit, just to please me, but I could see the shine going from his fur, and his sparkly, wise old eyes got dimmer and dimmer.

'Well, son, I think this is it. My ninth life coming to an end. I've taught you everything I know. Now it's up to you. You learned well, and you'll survive. But remember what I told you. Get yourself a person, and don't leave it too long.'

There was nothing I could do for him. One night he just went to sleep and didn't wake up. I covered his body with stones, and put a few wild flowers on top. That was the first time in my life I cried. I loved Old Charlie.

I tried to get along on my own, but I was still very young. Somehow without Old Charlie there, I didn't get enough food, and I was soon very thin. I struggled on for about a month, but things just got worse and worse. I had something wrong with my ears, I picked up worms from some rotten food, my fur was starting to fall out, and I had a fight with a dog who bit off the end of my tail. All in all, I was doing very badly. But really, what got me in the end was loneliness. As long as I had Charlie, I had a family, and he was right - every cat needs a family.

I inspected quite a few people before I chose Jess, but none of them came up to Charlie's standards. I watched her for a week before I made a move, just to make sure, but I could tell she was lovely as soon as I saw her. Great big smiley eyes, and the gentlest voice I ever heard. I didn't have to put on an act to get in, because I looked pretty dreadful by then. If you saw me now, you would never think it was the same cat. I crawled up to her when she opened the back door one morning.

'Oh, you poor little darling! What has happened to you,' she said, picking me up and starting to stroke me. I managed to raise a faint purr, and looked at her all gooey-eyed. I didn't have to pretend, I loved her already. 'Let's get you inside and have a look at you.'

As she carried me into the kitchen, a man came in.

'What have you got there, Jess? It looks like a half-dead rat.'

'It's a kitten, Richard. He's in a very bad way.'

I didn't much like being likened to a rat. Nasty, dangerous things they are.

The man had a nice voice too, and seemed very sympathetic. He came over and took me from Jess, and put me on the kitchen floor.

'You just take it easy, old son, and we'll see what we can do for you.'

'His tail needs some antiseptic, and he has canker in his ears,' Jess said when she had given me a brief examination. 'Get some lotion from the bathroom, darling, and we'll clean him up a bit.'

She was very gentle, and although the stuff they put on my tail stung like the devil, I knew it was good for me, and tried to bear the pain. They cleaned out my ears, and put some soothing liquid on my eyes, which was lovely. I felt like a new cat in no time.

'What he needs is a good feed,' Richard observed, which perked up my spirits no end. 'Some warm bread and milk, I think.'

I would have preferred a sausage, but was grateful for any small mercy.

That bowl of bread and warm milk was one of the best meals I ever had. I can savour it even now. Funny how some things stick in your memory.

After my meal and general clean-up, I was purring fit to burst, and they both laughed and petted me. I decided right then that these two were my people, my family, so it was time to inspect my new quarters.

'Look at the little blighter! Stalking about as if he owns the place already. Jess, I think we have a permanent guest.'

'I think he's lovely, and definitely a survivor. He must have had a terrible time.'

'Well, they do say black cats are lucky, and one can't have too much luck these days.'

'He has to have a name, darling. What shall we call him?'

'I think he should have a name to live up to,' Richard said thoughtfully. 'Something strong and fearless. Perhaps he'll grow into it!'

They came up with quite a few suggestions, and I quite fancied Winston, in honour of our great leader. After a while, they got a bit silly, and Tarzan was mentioned, and Hannibal, neither of which appealed to me at all. Eventually, Jess suggested Samson, the strongest man in the world, which they both liked, and so did I. By the end of the day I was Sam, and Sam I shall stay until the day I die. Just as I shall love Jess and Richard until the day I die.

I had learned well from Old Charlie, and quite early on, I appropriated the best chair, the best bit of rug, a place on the bed, and in cold weather, the spot directly in front of the fire. Charlie told me it is a feline tradition to make sure of these things before rules are introduced banning one from the furniture.

It was not hard to love them, and I was devoted to Jess. When she went out I made a commotion, when she returned I gave her a rapturous welcome. When she sat down I sat on her, or near her. It wasn't an act to get extra titbits, I had been saving up love for as long as I could remember, and had only been able to give any of it to Old Charlie.

It took Jess a little while to get me into shape. There was medicine to be taken, some of which was not nice at all, I can tell you, and plenty of good food to be eaten, which was very nice indeed. There was also a visit to a person called a Vet, the horrors of which are best left unspoken. I made quick progress really, though, and filled out a treat.

'Sammy, you are the handsomest cat around here,' Jess said one day. 'Your fur has all grown back, and you are all muscle.'

I knew Jess was prejudiced, of course, because she loved me, but I must admit, without wishing to sound conceited, that I am quite dapper. I shall always be small, probably because of my bad start in life, but what I lack in size, I make up for in cunning. Old Charlie taught me, you see, and Old Charlie was smart.

When I had been with Jess and Richard for about two months, I was poking around at the bottom of the garden when I heard faint noises coming from under the hedge. There was all sorts of bits of rubble and old dead plants, so I had to dig my way through to find out what it was. I could hardly believe my eyes! It was two tiny kittens! They were very young, and only just had their soft little squealing noises. I could tell they had been left alone for a long time, because they had not been cleaned up, and a mother always keeps her kittens clean. Perhaps something had happened to her, just like something had happened to my Mum. They were starving, and I didn't know what to do. I couldn't feed them. Jess will help them, I thought, and I rushed around the hedge making as much noise as I could. It was enough to wake the dead. I may be small, but there is nothing wrong with my voice! Eventually, Jess came down to see what all the commotion was about.

'Sammy! For heaven's sake what's the matter? I thought you were being murdered!'

I showed Jess where I had cleared a path through to where the kittens were, and she bent down and picked them up, one in each hand.

'The poor babies. They must have been abandoned. They must be so hungry. We'll take them inside and try to get some milk down them. Come on, Sam, inside with you too.'

We put them on the kitchen floor, and while Jess warmed some milk, I gave them a good wash. They were so dirty, you could not even see what colour they were. No cat likes to be dirty, so a good clean-up made them feel better right away. They were brothers, sharing the same mother, but as sometimes happens in cat families, they had obviously had different fathers. One turned out to be a tabby. A bit like Old Charlie, but better marked. He had a big white bib, and a long white sock. He had amazingly long whiskers, so you could tell he would one day be a big, strong cat. If he got the chance to grow up. The other one was trouble right from the start. His fur was long, matted, and difficult to clean. He was a silvery gray colour, and had great almond-shaped green eyes. From his kitten-shape, I guessed he would be, when grown, a great big pudding of a cat. He wailed constantly, and as soon as any attention was given to his brother, clamoured and fussed until we took notice of him.

Eventually, we got them cleaned, fed and settled down in an old suitcase Jess lined with a blanket. At last peace descended, and I curled up in the suitcase with them for a nap. When Richard arrived home, they started up again, and he was ushered in to meet the source of the noise.

'Look what Sam found,' Jess said, showing Richard the two new members of the family.

'Well, they look a bit sorry for themselves. More abandoned orphans,' he said peering into the suitcase.

'You should have seen them before Sam cleaned them up. They looked just like two bits of used cotton wool. They're too young to lap, so I'm feeding them with an eye dropper.'

Richard was giving me a bit of a stroke and a tickle.

'I take it they are joining the household?'

'They will be company for Sam. Anyway, if we turn them out they will die, poor little things. There is too much death already without any more.'

I knew Jess wouldn't let me down. It would be lovely looking after them, and I would make sure they were never on their own like I was.

Jess had to feed them with the eye-dropper for about ten days, then they started to get a bit of strength, and the tabby clambered out of the suitcase for a look round. He came across my bowl, and after I had demonstrated, started lapping away as if he had always known how. The gray one just lounged about in the suitcase, expecting to be waited on hand and foot. When he wanted something, he just howled until he got it. They were quite a handful, and I tried to be both mum and dad to them. I was on the go all the time.

'That gray one reminds me of Colonel Butler,' Richard remarked one evening, after repeated howling had summoned Jess and me for the hundredth time. 'He wants to have everyone's full attention, and his own way in everything. Just like the old man.' Richard's Colonel was renouned as a single-minded and determined individual.

'Then we shall have to call him Butler,' Jess replied smiling. And so we did, but he soon became Butty, which seemed to suit him.

'Where are Sam & Co?' was Richard's first question on his return home each evening.

'Butty is eating as usual. Sam & Co. are asleep.'

In accordance with their rather wierd sense of humour, the tabby was christened Co. However, he soon became Cosie, or occasionally CoCo, which he has remained.

So, there we were. At last I had my family. Jess, Richard, Butty, Cosie and me. It was as if I had come home after a long and difficult journey.

* * * * *

I can never remember a time when Sam, Butty and Jess were not there. I have always been loved and cared for, for which I am very grateful. Sam told us all about being alone, and it does not sound to my taste at all.

Sam is my hero. He is such a good, wise cat, and has been like a father to me and my brother Butty. He is not much older than we are, but he had a very hard life until he found Jess. I would have liked to have met his friend Old Charlie. He sounds like a very fine cat. I know how lucky I have been. I have never known a day's loneliness or hunger in my life. I grew up to be big, strong and healthy, and although I say it myself, my coat is beautifully marked.

We have a splendid time in our house. Sam is full of good ideas for outings and things to do. Whenever we do something wicked and Jess and Richard are annoyed with us, Butty does one of his tricks and makes everything all right again. Butty can be exasperating at times. He can be sillier than anyone I know, and he eats like a pig. I'm very fond of him though. No-one is perfect.

I suppose you could call me a trifle on the serious, studious side. We taught ourselves to read by listening to Richard, who has a habit of reading aloud articles in the newspapers, and I spend a lot of my time in the Public

Library. I dodge the Librarian and head straight for the Reference Section. I usually have the room to myself; people do not have much time for study these days. I spend hours just browsing. It's a shame I can only reach the lower shelves, it has left a few gaps in our education. The Encyclopaedia Britanica is way out of my reach unfortunately. I pass on what I learn to Sam and Butty. Butty doesn't absorb much, unless it's about gourmet cooking, but Sam understands everything. If I am stuck on something, Sam comes down to the Library with me, and we work out the problem together.

My other passion is detective stories and murder mysteries. I usually work out who the killer is by about Chapter Four. It's a good intellectual exercise, and usually only a matter of applying the basic principles of logic. I always feel sorry for the poor policeman who is completely baffled by the case and has to have the whole thing explained to him by the amateur detective in the last chapter. Real policemen can't possibly be as stupid as they are in books, otherwise criminals would never get caught at all!

I am a very fastidious cat. Butty says I will wash myself away one day. I don't mind admitting that I am fur-proud. My white is always spotless, and my stripes always shining and ordered. We all have to look after Butty, who has trouble with his long fur. If left to his own devices, he would spend most of the time looking like a demented powder-puff.

'Cosie is a rather aloof cat, don't you think? Not at all like the other two.' Richard and Jess were discussing us and our various little idiosyncracies. 'He almost seems to ration the affection he lets you give him. Sam and Butty will take any amount of fussing, but Cosie just draws the line when he's had enough, and wanders off.'

'It's just his way, Richard. I'm sure he loves us just as much as Sam and Butty. He is just not a demonstrative animal.'

Jess got it right, of course. Just because I don't slobber all over everybody like Butty, or spend hours being stroked like Sam, doesn't mean I love the family any less. I know that Butty and I would be dead were it not for Sam and Jess. But I shall not try to be something I am not just to please everybody else. I am quite happy the way I am. Sam says you should be true to yourself, and I think he is right. I fit my fur, and have all I want from life. How many cats can say that?

* * * * *

I don't know why everyone thinks I am silly. Just because I don't understand Cosie's mathematics, or Sam's history and geography, doesn't mean that I am stupid. Those things just don't interest me. Cooking, now, that is another matter. I can tell you the recipe for Lobster Mousse or Chicken Kiev right off the top of my head, and quicker than Cosie can say his twelve-times-table.

What sometimes makes me seem silly, is my short-sightedness. I don't really see things clearly until I am right on top of them, so I am always bumping into this and that. It gives me a lot of problems.

I do not let it worry me. Aristocracy quite often suffer from slight physical defects, and in many cases, do not appear to be overly bright. I am, of course, part-pedigree. A friend of Richard's who came to tea recently confirmed what I had always suspected. Apparently the man is quite an expert on cats.

'Definitely half-Russian Blue that one, Richard old man. Possibly even a bit of Persian.'

'I wonder which bit!' Richard joked, not in the least awed by the discovery of my upper-class background.

I rather think my distinguished forebear was brought to England by a Russian Archduke fleeing from the Revolution. He probably had a below-stairs affair with a servant's cat, and the line was unfortunately diluted. However, breeding will out. It gives one a certain air, and one tends to attract attention and respectful affection.

'Butty, you are the most amazing snob,' Cosie said to me just last week when I was speculating upon the possibility of my ancestor having visited the great palaces at St. Petersburg. I know he is just jealous because he is a plain old tabby, and take no notice.

They may call me silly, but who is it who gets us out of trouble, I'd like to know? When we are in disgrace, it is I who grovels and enchants until we are forgiven. I have a whole range of tricks to make our people laugh. My personal masterpiece is my headbutt, which I accompany with loud squeaking noises. This has never been known to fail, even when we ate some meat Jess was about to cook for Richard's dinner. Well I suppose I ate most of it, to be perfectly truthful, but Sam and Cosie had a little bit. My rolling around the floor with my legs waving in the air trick is also quite successful, not to mention my twisting high leap in the air after flies. I have also perfected lying about in positions which make me look pretty, and which make people say 'Oooh, isn't he beautiful!' It is quite true, of course, I am extremely beautiful. It's my breeding. People love to love me, and

I love to love them. What's wrong with that? My idea of a cat's heaven is to be so full of food I could not manage another morsel, and to have someone stroking and fussing me all the time. Bliss!

My girlfriend Minnie doesn't think I am stupid. Minnie lives just down the road, and to me she is lovely. Cosie says she is too Botticelli for his taste, whatever that means. I think it has to do with being fat. But then I am fat too, so we suit each other. Minnie's fur is tortoiseshell, and quite short. She says she envies mine because it is so long and elegant - particularly my tail, which is like a big fan. I can understand her envy. Females like to be beautiful, and although it may sound conceited, it is true to say that I am more beautiful than any cat around here - even Minnie!

What does it matter if I am silly anyway ? I doubt there are many cats as happy as I, in the entire world. I would not leave my family to live in a castle - unless King George himself summoned me to Windsor, of course. No, love is what it is all about. Jess, Richard, Sam, Cosie and me, and I love them. I would die for any one of them if necessary. Noblesse oblige it is called. Throughout the centuries, knights and lords have died for the peasants. It is something that is handed down to you with your breeding.

CHAPTER FIVE
LOVING AND DYING

Love in wartime is frightening in its intensity. Each searingly brief time together could be the last. Like a flower subjected to intense heat and light, it flourishes in almost tropical splendour. There is no time for the petty quarrels of settled times; small irritations are of no consequence.

Jess and Richard delighted in each other. Their tiny house in Chelsea consisited of a living-room, kitchen, minute hall, and overgrown back garden. A narrow staircase led to the first floor, which boasted a bedroom, box-room, and bathroom.

'I think I shall convert this palatial and distinguished room into my study,' Richard said laughingly, standing in the middle of the box-room. It was so small, he could very nearly touch both sides when standing with his arms extended. 'Floor to ceiling bookshelves, of course, and a desk with matching swivel chair.'

'Very elegant, my darling,' Jess replied. 'The only problem being that with that lot in here, there would be no room for you!'

Jess spent hours scrubbing, painting, and sewing curtains and cushions. They haunted street markets, and together chose interesting ornaments and pictures, which made the house 'theirs'.

On one of their expeditions, they found a wicker cat-basket, which Richard thought would be ideal for Sam, Butty and Cosie. Jess had her doubts, which were fully realised when they got it home. It was put on the floor, and the cats rushed in as they always did to inspect new purchases. Sam and Cosie refused even to enter it, despite being coaxed with titbits. They looked haughtily at Jess and Richard, turned up their noses, and jumped up on their favourite chairs, feighning sleep. Butty sniffed at it, walked around it once or twice, then sat in the middle of it and peed. Butty always expressed extreme disapproval of something by peeing on it. The basket was put under the stairs, never again to see the light of day.

The house was a happy place, and Syd kept them supplied with the little delicacies which contribute so much to the enjoyment of life.

On the first anniversary of their meeting, Jess cooked a special dinner. Afterwards, they relaxed on the sofa, enjoying a glass of Syd's black-market brandy. They were talking quietly, making plans for after the war. Suddenly, Richard rose and started pacing around the the room.

'Jess there is something I have got to tell you. I want you to hear me out, without interrupting.'

Richard then confessed to Jess the other side of her gallant Army officer - the thief.

Sam, who had been dozing on Jess's lap, pricked up his ears and gave his full attention. He jumped down, stretched langourously, and went over to where the Cosie and Butty were asleep on the rug. He woke them quickly by the simple expedient of biting Butty's tail, and sitting on Cosie's head. A brief scrap ensued, during which he told them both to listen hard to the conversation between their people.

'So, as you can see, I am really a thoroughly bad lot, and should be put away. I wouldn't blame you if you kicked me out, but I hope you won't. I love you very much.'

Jess was plucking nervously at her fingers, and staring at Richard in disbelief.

'I should kick you out. It's a tremendous shock; something I never would have considered in my wildest nightmares. Me, a Vicar's daughter! Living in sin is bad enough. But living in sin with a burglar... my father must be spinning in his grave. Do you intend to continue this 'career' after the war, may I ask?'

'Yes Jess I do. It has given me a very good life, which I enjoy. I never hurt anyone, and everything I stole was covered by insurance. Besides, there's not just me to consider. There's you now, and what kind of life could I give you on Army pay? There's also Syd to consider. He depends on me. He told me not so long ago that lots of his villians have been killed already, and its far from over yet. And I haven't even mentioned that lot on the rug!' He gestured with a smile at the furry heap which was to all intents and purposes fast asleep, but which was following every word avidly.

'Please be serious Richard. If I understand you corrrectly, you intend to support me, Syd - and let's not forget the cats - on the proceeds of breaking and entering.'

'Basically that's it. I am what I am Jess. It's no good saying I will change, because I won't. The love of a good woman is not going to put me on the straight and narrow. I have been a burglar, and a very successful one, for years. I could say I will stop to make you happy, but I would be lying to you. I won't do that. Nor will I go back to being poor.'

The discussion went on and on. The furry heap abandonded all pretence of sleep, and followed each exchange in much the same way that spectators at a tennis match follow a ball.

Eventually a subdued silence enveloped the room, and Butty, who did not care how the money for his next meal was obtained, decided that enough was enough. He stalked over to them and did his never-fail trick of head-butting Richard's knees while squeaking loudly. As always, it did not fail. Laughter broke the tension and Jess was in Richard's arms, giggling and crying at the same time.

'I don't care what you are. I can't be without you. Even if you stole the Crown Jewels I would still love you. But please don't get put in prison. I couldn't bear to be apart from you.'

The next day they went to Brighton to see Syd, who thoroughly approved of Jess. They lunched sumptuously on Syd's black-market goodies, and were entertained by his stories of villains and their doings, and the second hand furniture business.

That Christmas of 1942 was the happiest Jess could remember. The war seemed to be something that was happening to other people, and they lived with Sam, Butty and Cosie in their private little world.

The only dark cloud on Jess's horizon was that the Army doctors had pronounced that Richard would probably be fit to return to active duty within a few months. She pushed this dark prospect to the back of her mind, and refused to allow reality to intrude on her perfect contentment.

In fact it was six months before he was fit, and in June 1943, the Army reclaimed him for the invasion of Sicily.

It was six months before she saw him again.

During these months, Jess worked as an Auxilliary Nurse, and found out what exhaustion truly was. The strain of watching the young men die and comforting their families left her physically and emotionally drained. She lived for Richard's letters and crossed each day off the calender as one less she would be without him.

He came home for a brief leave in December 1943, and they spent Christmas quietly at home with the cats. Syd came on Christmans Day, bearing a turkey, and all manner of half-forgotten treats.

As he was leaving, Syd voiced his worries about Richard's survival.

'There's always some way to fiddle a nice, safe posting, but will he do it? Not on your Nellie! He's more than done his bit, and his luck can't last forever. He used up plenty when he was doing the burglaries.'

Love in wartime is frightening in its intensity. Each searingly brief time together could be the last. Like a flower subjected to intense heat and light, it flourishes in almost tropical splendour. There is no time for the petty

'Well, any time you need me, love, you know where I am.'

For the rest of that brief time together, they hardly left the house.

Richard was exuberent and boisterious, there were rough-and-tumble play fights with the cats, and everything was treated as fun.

Having accepted that Richard was an incorrigible burglar, Jess wanted to know all about the things he had done. He told her everything. How he planned and executed his robberies, how to crack a safe, how to beat alarm systems. Although he had never worked with anyone else, he told her how he would have used an accomplice to create a diversion if necessary. He told her how to leave no clues, how to get in, and more importantly, how to get out.

He told her that the war years had used up all his savings. He didn't mention that the families of his men killed in action had received a handsome cheque with his letters of condolence. That was private. That was between him and the dead.

'Never mind. As soon as things settle down a bit I'll be back in business, and we'll be set up in no time.'

'After my graduate course, I could set up on my own if I had the nerve,' laughed Jess, knowing that she would be incapable of stealing so much as a comb from Woolworth's.

And we could set up on our own too, mused Sam and Cosie, who had not missed one word. Butty, upon discovering that the subject matter was not food, had slept throught he entire lecture.

All too soon, Richard's leave was over, and each happy hour became a memory to be jealously hoarded away.

Jess somehow got through 1944. When the D-Day casualties came into the hospital in June, she frantically asked all the wounded men if they had seen him, and was rewarded by news from a blinded lieutenant that he was safe.

There was a brief week's reunion in Novermber 1944, and they were happier than they had ever been before. Then again back to the fighting, back to the death, back to the horror.

On the first of May 1945, a week before peace finally came to an exhausted Europe, Jess opened the door to a stocky man in Khaki wearing a major's crowns on his shoulders. She knew immediately, and held on to the door for support. He helped her to an armchair, and thought that no matter how many times you saw this particular dessolation, it never became any easier.

'Richard left a letter. Didn't want you to get one of those telegram thingies.' He fiddled uncomfortably with his hat.

She could not cry yet. That release would come later, in private.

'How did it happen?'

'It was one of those Hitler Youth kids. No more than thirteen. Stood there with a bloody machine pistol and blasted four blokes to hell. Richard was the first to get it. Couldn't have known a thing. I'm most awfully sorry. Can I do anything for you?'

'No. No, nothing, thank you. I'd like to be on my own now please.'

The major left, closing the door softly behing him.

Jess stared unseeingly at the envelope addressed to her in Richard's almost incomprehensible scrawl.

Butty and Cosie were out on various errands of their own, and Sam sat quietly at her feet, hoping to give some comfort by his warmth and nearness.

My darling Jess,

As you are reading this letter, it means that I am no longer around. The Constabulary will no longer be plagued by me, and the Army has lost so many, one more will not even be noticed.

I left this letter with Archie Cranston, who's a good sort of chap, and much better, I thought, than a telegram laddie.

First, I want to thank you for making me so happy these past few years. Now I want you to put me in my proper place. Cry some tears, and then bung me back in the old memory, and haul me out at Christmas and birthdays for a little wallow. Don't let me dominate the rest of your life. It's harder for the people left behind, it always is. I don't expect I knew much about it when it happened.

We had so much in our short time together. Much more than most people have in a lifetime. It will have to be enough.

There's only you and Syd to miss me. Go and see him for me Jess. He was a good friend. I expect those three mangy moggies might miss me a little, but they always had you firmly in first place. You tell them that I expect them to look after you now.

My biggest regret is that I have nothing to leave you. All my ill-gotten gains are gone long ago. Should have fitted in one or two jobs when I was on leave! Apart from that, no regrets Jess. I lived the way I wanted to, I found a woman to love with all my heart, and I didn't wind up limbless or crippled. I couldn't have borne that.

You had all my love Jess.

Richard

Then the crying started. She rushed into the bedroom and sobbed into his clothes, breathing the faint, man-smell of him that remained on them.

Sam read the letter she had left on the table. Yes, my old son, you were right, he thought. We will miss you, but she's our darling, and somehow we have to take care of her.

Two days later, the gasping, hysterical sobing was subsiding, and a numb acceptance was beginning.

The first day, she had decided to kill herself. She filled a bath with hot water, and took Richard's cut-throat razor with her into the steaming water. As she lay back in the comforting warmth, six paws appeared on the bath rim, swiftly followed by six stricken, fur-fringed eyes.

'Go away. I don't give a damn what happens to you. You'll have to fend for yourselves.'

Sam looked devastated, Butty squeaked, and Cosie looked resigned. But they did not go away. Finally, she did not go away either.

Jess arrived in Brighton to find Syd's house locked and shuttered. A neighbour informed her, not without sarisfaction, that the police had taken him away the previous week.

She was allowed to see him the gloomy nick. He was destroyed by the news of Richard's death.

'What happened Syd? Is it very bad?'

Syd gave a rueful laugh. 'Well, they're trying to pin everything that's happened, since the Titanic went down, on me. Fencing, Income Tax, Black Marketeering - the bloody lot. Money's got to be spread around in big lumps, but with any luck, I'll get off with a couple of years. Be out in eighteen months with good behaviour. I'll be wiped out, though. Everything has got to be sold. Did Richard look after you - financially? Are you all right?'

'No, there's nothing. We spent it all when he was alive. I wouldn't have had it any other way. It isn't important.'

'What will you do? I wish I could help, but you can see how it is.'

'Oh, I expect we'll get by Syd. Don't worry. Will you let me know about the trial and what happens. I'll come and visit.'

They parted sadly, and once again Jess was on her own - well almost.

Syd did indeed get two years, and Jess visited him faithfully every month.

The following year was very tough. The hospital no longer required its wartime level of staff, so Jess returned to Lyons Corner House, and somehow managed to make ends meet. It was a struggle to pay the rent on the house, but it was so full of memories, she could not bear to lose it.

One of the kitchen ladies at Lyons became very fond of Jess, and surreptitiously provided her with scraps, which kept the wolf from the cats' door.

They survived.

CHAPTER SIX
THE CAT BURGLERS

Sam was worried about their deteriorating standard of living. Jess was too thin, and worried all the time. It seemed to Sam that her life was devoid of fun, and he knew this was not right.

One Saturday night they were in the old Anderson shelter mulling over the past.

'We just can't go on like this,' Sam announced for the hundredth time.

'It's all very well saying that Sam,' Cosie said stoically. 'What can we do; we're only cats. We can't replace Richard, so it's pointless talking about it.'

Butty was in his usual semi-comatose state, and yawned loudly.

'Cosie is right. Unless, of course, we become cat-burlars!' Butty giggled at his own joke.

Sam and Cosie looked at each other wonderingly.

'Oh come now,' Butty grinned. 'That idea is quite preposterous... well almost quite preposterous... no, it isn't preposterous at all! The cogs of Butty's brain tended to move somewhat ponderously. Sam and Cosie were ahead of him.

'But who would we rob? How would we do to? How would we spend the proceeds?'

'Don't worry your little brain with details, Butty.' Sam said, his brows contracting as he concentrated on the problems their new activities would generate. 'You can leave all that side of the operations to Cosie and me. All you have to do is follow instructions, and promise to refrain from heroics. Much as you would love to be, you are not, and never will be, Errol Flynn.'

'Oh I see. As usual I will be required only to fetch and carry, and do all the boring things you two consider beneath you. It really is unfair. In view of my pedigree, I should automatically be the leader, and it was, after all, my idea.'

'With you as leader, my dear Butty, we should undoubtedly have the shortest criminal career on record. If you remember, you were asleep all the time Richard was talking about being a successful thief. You wouldn't have the remotest idea of how to plan or execute a job. In addition, you haven't read any mysteries or whodunnits as I have, nor have you survived on your own, as Sam did.That alone taught him how to think quickly in an emergency and get himself out of tight corners.

Cosie sank down on his cushion and proceeded to re-order his stripes, which had become ruffled during his speech.

'Let's not start off by falling out!' Sam laughed, giving Butty a playful cuff on the ear. Each one of us has something to offer. We'll all be able to make useful contributions. That's why people have gangs; each individual looks at things from a different angle, and what one brain may miss, another will pick up. Anyway, we're family. We don't need a hierarchy of command. Just tell me when we ever disagereed about something important? Everything will be open to suggestion or amendment by all of us. One thing, however, is absolutely certain. At the moment, we are all a bit soft physically. Before we start being feline Robin Hoods, we have to get fit.'

'I absolutely agree, Sam,' Cosie muttered, battling valiantly with a last recalcitrant clump of fur which refused to lie in its appointed place on his beautifully marked rump. 'We have a very easy life. Jess coddles us, and we let her. It's time we sharpened up our instincts and reflexes. I almost lost a fight last week with that wretched dachshund of Mrs. Tilbury's. I thought at the time that I was not as tough as I used to be.'

'Get fit! Me?!' Butty was round-eyed with apprehension and horror. 'Do you mean lose weight? Stop eating? Exercise? This is too much! I'm as keen as anyone, but there are certain things which are sacrosanct. My food, for example.'

'Sacrifices have to be made initially. Undoubtedly when we are on a sound financial footing again, Jess will spoil us dreadfully. Then you can eat yourself to death and no-one will mind. For now, however, we will all embark on a programme to turn us into lean, hungry killers.'

'Sam is right,' Cosie concurred, 'although I don't think it will actually be necessary - or feasible - to kill anyone. You're out-voted Butty!'

In the early days at the house in Chelsea, Richard had regaled them with tales of his days at Sandhurst and various Army garrisons. Sam now recalled a hilarious account of Richard supervising training which had included a mock assault course. Apparently nervous recruits had been required to swing on ropes, crawl through oversized pipes, climb walls, and cope with various other tortures designed to strengthen the backbone and tone up the muscles.

That's just the kind of thing we need to get into shape, Sam thought. After all, we are a kind of recruit, albeit in a very different Army to that which took an oath of loyalty to God, King and Country.

During the war, a nearby branch of Barclays Bank had been the loser in an encounter with a large German bomb. The great financial institution was in the process of rebuilding its off-shoot, and the site was covered with piles of sand and cement, scaffolding, planks of wood, coils of rope, and all the chaos which seems to be a necessary part of building anything. It was agreed that here was their ready-made gymnasium, and they went to bed early in order to make an early start the following day, when the site would be empty of workmen.

'Right,' Sam said briskly upon arrival. 'A few runs up and down that sandhill will do for starters. That should get our blood pumping nicely.'

The sandhill was about six feet high, and tough to climb with no paw-holds. Sam and Cosie easily managed the prescribed six runs, but after two excruciatingly slow efforts, Butty sprawled face down, gasping for breath.

'I'm going to be sick. I'm going to die. This is torture! I'll never get up and down here six times.' His pink tongue was hanging out, and his fat chest was heaving.

'You can't expect to get fit all at once,' Cosie comforted him. 'Two will do for today; tomorrow night you can do three.'

The next likely looking obstacle was a long plank of wood suspended about three feet above the ground betweeen two metal drums.

'Six across, and six back,' Sam commanded. 'No creeping mind, speed and agility are the goals.'

The plank was suspended above a shallow pool of muddy water, and needless to say, the inevitable happened. On his first, fast (for him) run, Butty fell off the plank and plopped chest-deep into the murk.

'This is just too much,' he wailed. 'I refuse to have anything more to do with this stupid nonsense. What's the good of being fit if you've killed yourself in the process? I'm going home to have my breakfast, and try to forget these nightmares.'

It took Sam and Cosie a while to calm Butty down, and get some of the mud off his fur. Eventually he was persuaded not to give up, and to tackle the rest of the training.

The builders had sectioned off various areas of the site with heavy tape suspended on wooden pegs a little way off the ground. They all grabbed a fairly heavy stone in their mouths, and proceeded to belly their way under the tapes. Butty found it hard to hold his stone and keep his head down at the same time. Having successfully negotiated two lines of tape, he was so pleased with himself he raised a paw to wave at Sam, got tangled up, and had to be extricated by the other two.

'If that had been an alarm wire,' Cosie admonished, 'we'd have had half the cops in London here before we could get you out. You really must learn to think Butty.'

They climbed and jumped, balanced and ran all the morning. Finally, when Sam and Cosie were tired, and Butty was at the point of collapse, they went home for their Sunday lunch. On arrival, Butty was subjected by Jess to the final indignity of a bath, to remove the caked mud and sand from his fur.

They slept like the dead all afternoon and all night, and Jess wondered what on earth they had been up to.

They awoke stiffly the next morning. Butty asserted that he was absolutely unable to move, would probably never be able to move again, and that on the whole he thought death was preferable to exercise. However, the lure of breakfast proved too strong, and eventually he staggered into the kitchen for his meal, and started on the slow path to recovery.

It took ten visits to the building site before it was agreed that they were in a fit state for their new profession. Butty was pronounced to be as ready as he would ever be, and it only remained to decide on their first contributor.

They all shared an intense dislike of the local newsagent. Arthur Trent was an obese, sweaty man, with a loud voice, and hard, tiny eyes which just managed to peep out of his fleshy face. In addition to selling newspapers and magazines, he was the local bookmaker, and loaned money at incredible rates of interest. Once indebted to him, it was almost impossible to get free.

At the back of his shop was a small yard containing dustbins and other clutter, surrounded by a high brick wall with broken glass set in the top, and overlooked by a tree.

Our trio of potential outlaws kept watch on Arthur Trent for a few weeks. It appeared that he had several runners working for him, who delivered their money and bets daily.

Arthur had an unusual safe for his bets and his money. A brick at the base of the yard wall had a piece of wire protruding from it. The wire would not be noticed in the normal course of events, but the surveillance team, comfortably ensconced and almost invisible in the tree, was not exactly normal. In this apparently safe place, Arthur kept a bag containing his betting slips and stake money, his shop takings, loan repayments and loan records. Every Sunday evening, he exchanged a full bag for an empty bag, and on Monday morning spread his profits around several bank accounts. His official bank account showed that the newsagent's shop made very little profit. He had a healthy respect for the Inland Revenue, and did not intend to get caught out by them.

A planning meeting was held in the Anderson on the Thursday night. In spite of Butty's original protests, Sam automatically became Chief Planner, Cosie was in charge of logistics, and Butty was detailed as lookout and general labourer.

'It's all very simple but for one thing.' Sam was pacing about as he always did when he was thinking aloud. 'The glass on the wall is no problem, so it's up the three, onto the wall, and straight down into the yard. What we have to work out is how to get the moneybag over the wall and back home.'

'Why bring the bag at all?' Cosie put in. 'Why don't we open it there, and just ferry the money home in several batches?'

'We could do that, but it increases the risk of our being seen if we make several trips backwards and forwards with bundles of pound notes in our mouths.'

They all rolled about laughing as Sam sketched a vision of the three of them in the dock at the Old Bailey like the villains in a film they had watched when they sneaked into the local flea-pit one wet afternoon.

Cosie came up with the solution. They would take their own bag, and leave it at the foot of the tree on the street side of the wall. When all the money was safely transferred, they would drag it home. The deed would be done on Saturday night to ensure a good haul.

At last the great night arrived. Pitch black, cold and windy. There would be few people about.

They waited in their house until 2 a.m. Jess was sound asleep. Butty was sent out to reconnoitre and reported that all was clear.

'It's a horrible night, and anyone with any sense is in their bed - which is where we should be.' Butty grumbled as they trooped out of the cat flap.

They quickly reached the hub of the Trent empire, and shinned nimbly up the tree, having deposited their carrier bag at its base. Sam and Cosie flipped lightly onto the wall, and down into the yard. Butty was left in the tree, and cautioned to give warning if anyone approached.

They located the wire, and Sam got a good grip on it with his teeth.

'It's no good Cosie, it's hardly moving at all,' Sam hissed.

'Just keep going Sam. It's got to move. Give it a bit longer, then I'll take over.'

In fact, it took them a wearying hour before a gap big enough to accommodate a paw was created. Then it was easy. They just dragged the brick out, and there it was: the week's riches of Arthur Trent lay revealed. They quickly made a neat pile of the betting slips and loan records, and another neat pile of the money.

Cosie jumped to the top of the wall with a mouthful of money, and instructions for Butty to join the transportation team. Butty was sound asleep and snoring softly.

'You bloody idiot!' Cosie spat furiously. 'You could have got us all nicked!'

'Sorry Cosie, but you were such a long time. I must have just dozed off,' Butty whispered. 'I'll get down and help with the money.'

It didn't take long for the transfer to be effected, conveniently most of it was crisp, white £5 notes, and was not too bulky.

Butty sat on their now valuable carrier bag, while Sam and Cosie tidied up in the yard. It was easier to get the brick back in placer than it had been to get it out.

'What shall we do with the bets and loan records? It would be nice to destroy them. Old Trent wouldn't know where he was.' Cosie hated to leave loose ends.

'There's a bucket full of rainwater over there,' the ever resourceful Sam pointed out. 'We could just drop the lot in and all he would find would be a mushy heap.'

The records were duly consigned to a watery grave.

They had left quite a few paw-prints, and remembering Richard's admonition to leave no clues, rolled around in the dust to obliterate them.

A final check showed the yard to be just as it had been when they arrived, except for the mush in the bucket.

They rejoined Butty on the other side of the wall. In an attempt to atone for falling asleep, Butty was guarding the carrier-bag with fierce concentration.

It was about 500 yards to their house, and they took turns to drag the bag. Butty did the lion's share, since Sam's and Copsie's gums were sore from dragging the wire. At last they dragged their precious cargo through the cat-flap, and collapsed on the kitchen floor. They heaved a collective sigh of relief, and then all started gabbling at the same time.

Butty, as ever the exhibitionist, rolled on his back kicking his legs in the air shrieking 'We did it! We did it! We did it!' Cosie purred contentedly, and Sam did little leaps up and down.

When they calmed down, they spread the money over the floor, and were astonished at the size of their haul. £400 made a very satisfying crackley noise when you walked over it; even more so when you rolled on it.

They had decided to trust in Jess's good sense, and just leave the money on the table. They felt sure she would not look a gift-horse in the mouth, also that she would have learned enough from Richard not to go blabbing around the neighbourhood, or spend large sums of money she was not supposed to have.

That astonishing Sunday morning, Jess slept late, and the trio were in an agony of excitement waiting for her to come and discover their bounty. Eventually, Jess padded into the kitchen wrapped in her dressing gown, and the accumulated fatigue of a week's waitressing.

She filled the kettle and put it on the stove, pottered about making toast, and generally luxuriated in the lack of a firm timetable for the day.

The cats seemed unusually agitated. She almost tripped over Butty twice as he wove in and out of her legs. Sam was purring and stalking up and down, and even Cosie was rubbing against her legs. They are a comfort, she thought. The house would be so empty without them.

At last, she took her tea and toast into the living room. As she was about to put her breakfast on the table, she spotted the unbelievable sight of a pile of money right in the middle of it. Sam jumped up and sat on the money; Cosie and Butty regarded it gravely from two chairs they had leapt on. Then they all turned their eyes on her, and she could have sworn they were twinkling.

'Where on earth did this come from?' She turned the money over with the puzzled joy of someone who has lost a penny and found a pound note.

Cosie and Butty joined Sam on the table, and they sat in a line like three Egyptian statues, staring at her steadily. They were never, never allowed on the table, and this was the only rule they usually respected.

'You got it! You found it! Somehow you got it! No, you can't have. Where? How...?' The exclamations and questions gushed out.

Sam jumped down and trotted to the bedroom. He brought back with him a pair of Richard's cufflinks which Jess kept on her dressing-table with other odds and ends of his, and dropped them on the money.

'No. Richard is dead. It cannot be from him. What are you trying to tell me? You got the money the same way as Richard got things? You stole it! This is impossible. I must be going mad. Cats do not go around stealing money!' She looked incredulously from one to the other. Sam pushed the money towards her, and laid a paw on her hand. He looked at her lovingly, and she knew. She knew that these three animals had stolen the money. God only knew how and from where, but they had stolen it.

'There must be hundreds here.' Jess counted rapidly. 'There's £400!' Cosie looked proudly at Sam, seeking acknowledgement of his mathematical genius.

They all jumped on her, and she was submerged in a furry avalanche of purring bodies. Butty managed to get in a couple of headbutts, then disengaged himself to deal with the forgotten toast. Butty hated waste.

They had unpicked the upholstery on the underside of an armchair, and Sam showed her their improvised safe by taking a £5 note and stuffing it out of sight. Jess put the whole bundle inside, and re-stitched the material.

'It's no good Cosie, it's hardly moving at all,' Sam hissed.

'There. No-one will ever find that. Even if we have burglars!'

Jess was more light-hearted than they had seen her since Richard's death. She kept picking them up for a cuddle, and giggling and laughing like a schoolgirl.

Butty could stand any amount of this, and Sam purred and licked her chin indulgently. Cosie, however, had had enough after an hour or so, and went out. He mooched around the neighbourhood for a while, had a good sleep in the Anderson, saw a couple of friends and had a bite to eat. Later he went and settled himself comfortably in the tree overlooking Arthur Trent's yard. He had been part of the cause; he wanted to see the effect.

Trent came to the yard at his usual time. He squatted his great bulk in front of his favourite brick and tugged it out. He felt inside the cavity as he had done a hundred times before, and found only an empty bag. He was so surprised, he overbalanced and fell backwards, right into a heap of waste products that Butty had felt obliged to deposit there the previous night.

'Bloody hell,' roared Arthur Trent. 'I've been done!'

He scrambled over to hoist himself up, and managed to further take advantage of Butty's generosity all over the knees of his Sunday suit.

'What's up Arthur?' Trent's wife Edna came running through to the yard, concern and apprehension distorting her already ugly features.

'We've been robbed. That's what's up! Everything's gone. The money, the bets, the loan records, everything. Nobody knew about the brick. Nobody... Not even you.'

'We'd better call the rozzers Arthur. They'll get it back sure as eggs is eggs.'

'Don't be a bloody fool, Edna. It was betting money and loan money, and they're both illegal. Do you want me to end up in the nick?'

Edna privately could think of worse things to happen, but wisely said nothing.

Arthur's face was contorted with malevolence. He stalked around the yard, swearing terrible retribution on his unknown enemy.

Then he spotted the bucketful of mushy papers. From one semi-legible particle, he ascertained that here was the final resting place of his precious records. If possible, he became even more angry, and vowed even greater and more horrible vengeance.

'I've got to go and see Percy. We'll have to sort out the bets.'

Trent slammed out of the yard, and puffed off down the road, followed at a safe distance by Cosie. He knocked agitatedly on the front door of a miserable house three streets away.

The door was eventually opened by a weasly little man, who turned out to be Percy. Percy had evidently been sleeping off the previous night's jollities, and was none too happy to be disturbed.

'We've got to talk. There's been a disaster. All the betting slips and loan records have been nicked.' Trent was almost exploding with rage. 'Get hold of Harry, Fred, Jack and Bill, and meet me at the yard in half an hour.'

'Gawd, who'd do a thing like that?' Percy said, thinking that off-hand he could come up with about fifty names. 'We'll be there Arthur. I'll go and get the others.'

As Trent charged off, Cosie saw a small smile light up Percy's thin face.

'We'll be there all right, Arthur,' he muttered, 'but first we've got a bit of figuring to do.'

Percy adjourned to the kitchen table, and Cosie to the kitchen window-sill. He spread out the Sunday paper, open at Saturday's racing results. There were two winners at 10/1, three at 6/1, and one really lucky shot at 40/1, which was so far behind when everything else in the race collapsed in a heap at the last fence, that it avoided the carnage, and recorded a completely unexpected triumph. So unexpected, its owner had suffered a heart attack, and had been removed to hospital.

Amongst Percy's regular punters, were several close friends, who would like nothing better than to put one over on the unlovely Trent. They would be in for a cut.

Percy rushed round to his colleagues to impart the good news, and each had thoughts along not dissimilar lines.

Muzzy brains shook off Saturday night hangovers, and plans were laid to take Arthur Trent to the cleaners.

Stan, whose dislike of the bookmaker knew no bounds, also had the good idea of dropping the word that the loan records were lost. Thus, lots of people would benefit. Outstanding amounts would be drastically reduced at a stroke. Stan intoned a silent benediction for the unknown thief.

Arthur and his runners duly assembled in the yard, and the true magnitude of his misfortune was revealed.

'I'm ruined,' he moaned scrutinising the lists compiled by his employees.

'Oh, come on Arthur,' said Percy, trying to keep the mirth out of his voice. 'It's just a bit of bad luck. You'll soon make it up. Can't win 'em all, old son.'

Arthur knew he was being taken, but there was absolutely nothing he could do about it.

On his way home, Stan stopped for a pint at the Prince Albert. He knew that the best way to spread anything around the district was to tell it in confidence to Doris, the barmaid. Within an hour, everyone in the Pub knew, and by Monday morning everyone in the surrounding area knew, by Monday evening, Jess knew.

'So that's where you got it,' she chortled. 'What a hoot! If Arthur Trent knew, he'd hang himself.' Sam just purred.

They had a meeting in the Anderson that night, and indulged in a great session of mutual congratulation.

They agreed to rest on their laurels for a while, and not push their luck. Jess had treated them to a large lump of Rock Salmon that evening, and they were relaxed and replete.

'Who says crime doesn't pay?' Cosie drawled, and they all giggled.

After a little nap, they went off to beat up a strange Tom, with more courage than sense, who was spending more time than was wise in their territory.

Jess didn't make the mistake of spending large sums of money she wasn't supposed to have. She bought little things to make life easier, but always did her buying in other districts.

The cats restricted themselves to intelligence gathering. Cosie and Sam sharpened their wits, and Butty grew fatter and fatter. They had enjoyed their first venture into crime enormously, and saw no reason why success should not bless their future endeavours.

Richard would have been proud of them.

CHAPTER SEVEN
MOVING UP - MARKET

About a month after the Trent episode, Jess came home with great news.

'Sid's coming out,' she told them. 'He's coming to stay until he gets on his feet.'

Sid's Black Market contributions to the wartime larder had earned him several of their gold stars, but it had been a long time since they had seen him, and they were undecided whether it was wonderful or not.

It took him about half an hour to win them over. He told Jess about cats he had been owned by in the past, fussed Butty into a state verging upon delirium, and admired Cosie's markings and Sam's intelligent head.

'You seem well Jess,' Sid observed, sipping his tea.

'I get by. We keep each other going,' Jess smiled, stroking the team who were at her side on the sofa.

'You need someone to look after you. Some nice young man must be around somewhere.'

'Oh I am looked after, Sid. But perhaps not in the way you think. The cats look after me, and I don't want a nice young man. No-one will ever replace Richard. What will you do? Get back to fencing?'

'Like a lot of people, I've got to start again. I'm going back into the second-hand furniture business first. But travelling this time, buy in the country, and sell in London. Call myself an antique dealer. I'll have to be careful. I've got form now, so I'll have to have some visible means of support. Got to get new contacts too. Bloody war ballsed everything up.'

'Yes it did, didn't it.' A bright flash of tears appeared in her eyes.

'I'm sorry Jess. Didn't mean to re-open old wounds.'

'It's all right Sid. You are the only person with whom I can talk about him. I can't go through life crying at the mention of his name. You and I are just two of the millions of small casualties at least we are alive.'

'Well, one thing is certain. You cannot stay here forever. You'll go on waitressing and living on memories and just shrivel up.'

'I have been thinking about that a lot. I've managed to save some money,' she blushed at this fib, 'and I am going into business.'

This little bombshell caused Sam to fall off the sofa, and Cosie to stiffen with shock. Butty didn't hear, he was asleep on Sid's lap.

She picked up Sam and stroked him.

'I have only just decided really. There is a little café for sale in Kensington, just behind Harrods. I am going to make it into a tea-shop, just like the old-fashioned ones years ago. I think I should get quite a nice class of customer.'

Jess looked pointedly at Sam, who could not decipher her plans at all.

'There is a little flat above, and a garden at the back, so I shall be able to take the tribe with me. They can potter about and enchant the customers. Sam was disgusted. He had no intention of enchanting anyone. He was a fully fledged burglar, and his contribution to the family coffers would be made that way. He had heard plays on the radio featuring the sort of rich, silly women Jess anticipated serving, and their endless chatter about parties, furs and jewellery bored him. Endless chatter about furs and jewellery. Furs and jewellery. Jewellery! Sam's brain slipped into top gear. Sid was free. Sid was a fence. Jesus Christ, they were going into business!

Sam looked up at Jess with perfect understanding. It was a peach. They were moving up-market. He went into an ecstasy of purring, and licked Jess's chin, as he always did when she pleased him. Jess and Sid laughed.

The greater part of Arthur Trent's donation was still intact, but a meeting in the Anderson decided that a top-up was necessary before they moved into the rarefied atmosphere of Kensington.

Solly Bernstein was a jolly, roly poly man. He lived a few streets away in a slightly better area, in a very desirable little bungalow. From the outside it looked like any of its neighbours, but Solly had turned the inside into a veritable little palace.

Solly was what was then known as a spiv. Anything you wanted, Solly could get. For a price - in cash.

'The problem is to find out where he keeps the cash,' Sam said to his co-conspirators at the planning meeting.

'There is only one way that I can see, and that's through his wife's horrible Siamese. She has been nursing a passion for Butty for years.' Cosie sat back and waited with amusement for Butty's reaction.

'No. Absolutely no.' Butty was appalled. 'That cat is horrible. She's stuck up, conceited, and stupid. Besides, Minnie would kill me.'

'There is no other way Butty. Sacrifices have to be made. In any case, when we move to Kensington you won't be able to see Minnie any more, so she will just have to get used to it.' Sam was unsuccessfully trying to keep a straight face.

'You could regard it as an undercover operation like in that film we saw last week, where the hero seduced the beautiful German temptress in order to get the coding machine.'

Cosie was playing on Butty's addiction to war and spy films. Butty had never understood why the Allies had not used cat-power for message carrying and infiltration. Nobody ever noticed a cat. He had even had fantasies of being parachuted into Berlin with an explosive collar and blowing up the Führer. A kind of kamikaze kitty!

'I suppose one's duty is one's duty,' he finally sighed. 'But I want you all to know I think this is above and beyond the call.'

'We'll award you a Victoria Cross afterwards,' Sam promised, and they worked out the strategy to obtain the unknowing assistance of Sheba, Mrs. Bernstein's horrible Siamese.

The seduction was easy, and in a post-passionate moment under Butty's skilful questioning, Sheba revealed that Solly was a very careful man. The only time he had money in the house was on Sunday nights. This was the proceeds of his dealings on Saturday and Sunday when the banks were closed. Her person was a very clever man, Sheba boasted, and made a great deal of money. This he kept in his wallet during his waking hours, and under his pillow when he was sleeping.

'There are such dreadful people about these days,' Sheba simpered. 'One simply cannot be too careful.'

'Indeed,' Butty agreed, sweeping the ground with his tail so that Sheba would have a clean place to sit. 'The world is full of dreadful and dishonest people. One must be alert at all times.'

'Precisely. Cleanliness and Godliness are qualities one meets so seldom. Mr. Bernstein of course is a joy. Bathes every Sunday night, regular as clockwork. Never a single nasty smell from him. Mrs. Bernstein does have rather poor taste in perfume, unfortunately, but she tries so ard. I believe Mr. Bernstein married beneath his station, but she is very kind and naturally, adores me. One must make allowances.'

Butty received a hero's welcome when he returned to the Anderson.

'That was the worst time of my life!' he exclaimed dramatically, and settled with relief on his personal cushion.

Butty repeated everything he had gleaned from their unwitting accomplice.

'There is no cat flap, and Mrs. Bernstein makes sure that Sheba is inside the house before they go to bed. They close all the windows every night, because Solly is terrified of burglars.'

They mulled over the apparent impossibility of the robbery, each making suggestions which were rejected by the others for one reason or another.

Butty's suggestion was the most bloodthirsty and impractical. His plan was to hang the obnoxious Sheba from a tree in the Bernstein garden, and wait for her people to discover the body. In the resulting confusion, they could nip into the bungalow and be away with the money before anyone knew what was going on.

'We are not going to murder anybody,' Cosie said. 'Anyway, I don't know how to tie a hangman's noose.'

As usual, Sam solved the problem.

'Just repeat that bit about Solly's Sunday bath,' he instructed Butty.

The following Sunday, they watched the Bernstein house to confirm that Sam's idea would work.

Solly obviously enjoyed his bath, and treated his audience of two, seated in the front circle of the bathroom window, to a selection of songs made famous by Vera Lynn a few years before. As we were all about to meet again one sunny day, Solly emerged from the bath and wrapped himself in an enormous towel. He began his post-bath routine of cleaning his teeth, cutting his toe nails, and generally pottering about the way people do, but first, he opened the bathroom window to allow the steam to escape and the condensation to dry.

Mrs. Bernstein was at the kitchen door calling Sheba, who was otherwise engaged with Butty.

Satisfied, Sam and Cosie returned home, and decided that the next Sunday, the Bernstein finances would be somewhat depleted, and that their own would correspondingly increase.

Butty had to endure another week of torment with Sheba.

'The Christian martyrs had it easy compared to what I am suffering,' he wailed. 'All they had to contend with was a quick few rounds with an arena full of lions and tigers. Sheba would have come out the winner.'

As a vital part of the plan, Butty persuaded Sheba into a late-night tryst on the appointed Sunday evening.

'As you know, I cannot be very late returning home,' Sheba said in her prim and peevish way. 'Mrs. Bernstein worries about me so.'

'I know, my dear,' Butty responded soothingly. 'I just want to show you our little Den in the Anderson.'

The three had worked very hard blocking all the exit and entrance routes in the shelter except one. Once Sheba and Butty entered, he had only to trip a plank of wood to effectively seal them inside, or let them out.

Sam and Cosie repaired to the Bernstein garden, and peered through the bathroom window at Solly, who was engaged in his post-bath activities. As before, the bathroom window was open, and as before, the steam was escaping, and the condensation was drying.

Mrs. Bernstein was at the kitchen door vainly shreiking for Sheba, who by this time had been the victim of an 'accidental' wood slip, which had sealed her and Butty inside the Anderson.

'You stupid animal,' Sheba was screaming. 'I told you I had to get home.'

'Don't you worry dear, I will get us out.' Butty was ineffectually poking at bits of wood, waiting for a signal.

'Sarah, will you forget that bloody cat and come to bed.' Solly had finished his toilette, and was more than ready to call it a day.

'Something must have happened to her. She always comes when I call.' Sarah's voice was full of concern.

'She'll come when I bloody call, or stay out all night.' Solly stalked to the back door, and joined his big voice to his wife's.

They heard a loud cat-call nearby, but it wasn't Sheba. It was Cosie's signal to Butty that they were entering the bungalow through the bathroom window.

They went swiftly through to the bedroom, and quickly located Solly's fat wallet under his pillow. Cosie grasped it between his strong jaws, and they both dashed out of the bungalow the way they had come.

A second loud howl signalled to Butty that the deed had duly been done, and they were on their way home - well pleased with their night's work.

On hearing the second signal, Butty miraculously managed to shift the plank which had been barring the only exit, and he and Sheba escaped gratefully into the fresh air.

'I shall be in all sorts of trouble because of you and your silly Den. I never, ever want to see you again.' Sheba was at full whine level, and Butty devoutly hoped she would not change her mind.

Sam, Butty and Cosie re-assembled in the kitchen, full of excited chatter.

'It was a doddle,' Sam chortled. 'A perfect plan.'

'It's all very well for you two. You don't have to face Minnie.' Butty said glumly.

More practically, Cosie was counting the money.

'£285,' he announced. 'Not as good as old Trent, but quite acceptable. What shall we do with the wallet?'

'We'll dump it in his garden. These papers and notes will be of value to him, and we only wanted the money. Solly's quite a good sort really, and I did enjoy his singing.' Sam had no wish to be unnecessarily harsh on so pleasant a contributor to their funds.

Cosie picked up the, now lighter, wallet for its return journey.

'Be careful Cosie,' Sam cautioned. 'Solly may have called the police.'

There was indeed activity in the bungalow. It appeared that Solly thought he had misplaced the wallet. Cushions had been thrown from sofas, rugs had been pulled back, and an armchair had been pushed over on to its side.

Cosie quietly padded over to where the dustbins were, and placed the wallet nearby. He concealed himself in the hedge to see what would happen next.

Eventually, having torn the house apart, Solly decided to look outside. He found his wallet almost immediately.

'It's empty! They money's gone! Hold on a minute, there are little marks on the leather. It looks like teeth marks. Sarah! That bloody cat of yours is involved in this somehow....where is the damned thing?'

He stomped into the bungalow, and Cosie reflected that Sheba would pay dearly for those stolen moments with Butty. He hoped it had been worth it.

'Oh you angels!' Jess exclaimed when she awoke to find the night's haul on the table. 'This will pay nicely for the redecoration, and help furnish our little flat. You are all so clever! My darling boys!'

They indulged in a session of mutual adoration terminated by Jess leaving for work. She would do nothing suspicious like abruptly disappearing from the district following the two robberies and had tendered her notice at Lyons as required. Due to an unexpected legacy, she had explained.

Unexpected legacies are not nearly so unusual as people tend to think.

CHAPTER EIGHT
THE HEY DIDDLE DIDDLE

Jess bought the little greasy spoon she had found in a street behind Harrods, and turned in into an oasis of gentility. She crossed lace curtains over the windows, painted the walls and ceiling a pale rose, and with Syd's help and guidance, installed beams, and good old furniture. Its walls were lined with dressers displaying pretty china and glassware, and her eight tables were covered with fine linen tablecloths. There was an alcove with a pair of comfortable, chintzy armchairs and a coffee table for those desiring just a pot of tea or a soft drink.

The only difficulty Jess and Syd had with the building and decorating work, was avoiding the enthusiastic assistance of Butty. They would put him, they thought, safely out of the way, but inevitably he would turn up covered in paint, leaving tasteful designs of paw-prints all over the floor, or be discovered sitting comfortably in a bucket of mixed plaster. He was recovering from the pasting he had taken from Minnie over the Sheba affair, and was nursing a badly bitten ear. This, in his view, entitled him to be even more loved and cuddled than ever, regardless of the fact that everyone was frantically working to complete the conversion. Sam and Cosie kept very much out of sight, knowing that the months ahead would bring great excitement and exertion, and taking advantage of the lull to rest up and get fit.

At last everything was ready, and all that remained to be done was the selection of a suitable name.

'I feel it should have something to do with the cats,' Jess mused to Syd. 'They are, after all, going to be having a lot to do with it.' She omitted to tell Syd that they had also provided the money to buy it. She didn't think that Syd was ready for that particular item of news just yet.

'Well, a few names spring to mind. Cosie's Corner, for example. Or perhaps Butty's Buttery. How about Sam's Snackery?'

'They all sound a bit... oh, I don't know. Just not right.'

'Did Richard ever tell you how we met,' Syd asked.

'Yes. He overheard some people talking about you in a Pub didn't he?'

'Right. But did you know that the name of the Pub was The Cat & Fiddle?'

'No. I didn't know that.' Jess thought for a few minutes. 'How about if we took another line from the rhyme. The Dish and Spoon perhaps? No, that's not right either. I know. It cannot be anything other than The Hey Diddle Diddle. I like it. It sounds just right.'

Syd agreed, and The Hey Diddle Diddle was born.

Discreet advertisements were placed in those country magazines beloved of the English upper and middle classes, and posters were distributed to the local Women's Institutes.

Soon, Jess built up a good solid clientele. The Hey Diddle Diddle became something of an informal ladies' club for those who had been doing a little light shopping in Harrods or similar nearby emporia. The menu included muffins, crumpets, home-made scones and cakes. She offered light lunches and teas, and closed at eight o'clock.

The cats settled in quickly, although Butty missed Minnie terribly at first. They soon became very much a feature of the establishment. Sam found it was really quite easy to be enchanting, but Cosie, despite lessons from the other two, never really took to that part of the plan, and spent most of his time in the back room memorising information picked up by his more extrovert partners. Butty, with his great liquid eyes, fanlike tail and lopsided walk, was everyone's favourite - the star of the show. His Mark II diving headbutt was a particular source of entertainment, and his naturally affectionate and loving nature could melt the stoniest of hearts.

Mrs. Abercrombie-Smythe was one of their first regulars. On opening day she had sailed through the door swathed in expensive fur, having just survived a couple of hours of exhausting shopping. She was tall, and shaped somewhat like an inverted pear. Her iron gray hair was swept into a chignon, which served to emphasize her heavily jowled chin, and complementary pendulous earlobes. Her small round black hat was perched on the top of her head, much like an olive on the top of a two-day old, sagging egg mayonnaise. Her voice matched her imposing appearance, and Sam, Butty and Cosie could only commisserate with the unfortunate Mr. Abercrombie-Smythe, who had to live with it.

As they learned more of the lady, through rapt attention to her conversations with her friends, it transpired that Mr. Abercrombie-Smythe was, in fact, Colonel Abercrombie-Smythe, and spent most of his time in the Far East with his regiment. His wife was unfortunately unable to join him due to recurrent malaria, which she had contracted some years previously. The Colonel seemed, to Sam, Butty and Cosie, to be an eminently sensible man.

The lady lived nearby in one of those lovely old houses bequeathed by the Edwardians to their largely unappreciative descendants.

'So very nice, my dear, having somewhere to meet one's friends. Most places are so common these days,' Mrs. Abercrombie-Smythe gushed one afternoon when she was having a few words with Jess. 'And so near to everything. Such a bother getting to Fortnums now with all the traffic. I do so love your pussycats too. makes it all so homely. I had a Burmese myself, but he died recently.' Butty was sitting on her lap, and gazed up at her adoringly. 'A possible cat-flap here,' he thought. 'Definitely worth investigation'.

'I do believe dear Butty has fallen in love with me. He never leaves me. I shall have to take him home with me.'

Butty had a nightmare vision of living with Mrs. Abercrombie-Smythe, and jumped down immediately with panic in his heart. He called Sam into the back room, and requested that he be relieved of duty in this particular area of operations at once. Sam rolled around laughing and told Butty not to be so silly. Jess would never donate them to anyone, least of all to the redoubtable lady currently engaged in an attempt to demolish an entire lemon meringue pie.

Cosie followed Mrs Abercrombie-Smythe home one afternoon, and was gratified to note that there was, indeed, a cat-flap. The kitchen, however, was guarded by one of those ancient retainers who never seem to die, but just fade eventually into the wallpaper. She chased Cosie away with vehemence indicating a strong dislike of felines in general, and of those with the temerity to venture into her kitchen, in particular. Cosie had his suspicions about the circumstances of the demise of Mrs. Abercrombie-Smythe's Burmese, and said a silent prayer that his tormented soul was at rest. Fortunately, they learned from subsequent eavesdropping, this harridan enjoyed a night off - Tuesdays - so all was not lost.

Their first visit was for a good look round. There were all manner of lovely things in the house, representing the cultures of many different parts of the world, and evidencing the Colonel's untiring travels about the Empire in the service of the King.

A large portrait of the Colonel hung above the fireplace, for which he had posed in full dress uniform, complete with sword. His expression was one of nervous anticipation, as if he expected his wife to appear at any moment, and wished to be somewhere else before she did. He seemed to be a relatively small man, and when he tried to imagine the couple together, Sam was reminded of a picture he had seen in a local gallery depicting a frigate dancing attendance on a great three-decker ship of the line.

Naturally, the fine silver and porcelain were too bulky for our diminutive band. They knew, however, that they had struck gold in the master bedroom. It was a lofty room, which couldn't make up its mind whether to be feminine and pretty, or masculine and functional. It therefore failed dismally on both fronts. On the feminine and pretty side, there was a dressing table which Cosie unhesitatingly identified as French. 'One of those Louis,' he said appraisingly 'but I'm not sure which.' The centre drawer was locked, and a five-minute intensive search revealed the key to be imaginatively concealed in the tulip-shaped glass shade of an Art Deco lamp.

Cosie had spent many hours at home practising his skills as a locksmith. He had developed the knack of manipulating keys with his jaws, and having inspected both key and lock closely pronounced there would be no problem.

'We'll just check that this is where she keeps the sparklers,' Sam said. 'We want to be in and out quickly when we lift them.'

There had been a slight hitch in the supply of a necessary item of equipment, so they were unable to complete the job. They felt confident that the obstacle would have been overcome by the following Tuesday, and that the secrets of the slim leather cases in the drawer would then be revealed.

They parted as silently as they had arrived, well satisfied with their reconnaissance.

They were still familiarising themselves with the district, and on the way home spent some time admiring the window displays of the shops, inspecting restaurant menus, and poking about in interesting little nooks and crannies.

They stopped briefly in front of a furriers, which made them all feel uncomfortable. Butty was convinced that a red fox Cossack hat in the window had once been Arnold, a ginger tom who had lived close to their house in Chelsea, and been father to Butty's beloved Minnie.

The hitch which had prevented the final act in the Abercrombie-Smythe adventure, was the design and fabrication of leather draw-string pouches which Jess was making for them. The pouches needed to be wide rather than long, or when full, the cat-burglars would be tripped by their burdens. After much experimentation, Jess got the proportions right, and each pouch could carry a satisfactory number of small items. Small valuable items.

As expected, the pouches were operational by the following Tuesday, and were left by Jess on the mantlepiece in case they should be required.

That night, a well-lit house revealed Mrs. Abercrombie-Smythe to be at home, and mission had to be abandoned. Frustratingly, and somewhat inconsiderately they thought, she was there again the following Tuesday.

Third time lucky. The house was empty, and the three stole quietly through the cat-flap, up the stairs, and into the bedroom. It was a matter of only moments before the drawer was opened, and the leather cases were revealed. All the cases were removed from the drawer, and spread out, open, on the carpet. Since their carrying capacity was limited, it was important that they selected the best pieces.

The Abercrombie-Smythe taste in jewellery was mainly for large stones in fairly plain settings suspended from gold chains. Not too heavy, and very portable. There were several splendid rings, including a stunning square-cut emerald, which they stowed in Sam's pouch. Being the smallest, Sam was permitted to carry less, his contribution being more in the area of planning.

A beautifully wrought golden serpent bracelet with ruby eyes gave them some difficulty. They solved the problem by winding it around Cosie's neck. Butty thought it looked better on Cosie than it would on their benefactress. The finest items in the collection were a matching necklace and bracelet of diamonds and sapphires. Butty was overjoyed. He had conducted a long and enduring love affair with sapphires ever since Sam had pointed out their calm, blue beauty in the window of a jewellery shop in Chelsea. He packed the necklace and bracelet into his little bag with glee. A heavily laden gold charm bracelet was loaded into Cosie's pouch, together with an intricate lace-like gold collar, whose origin was obviously oriental. Sam had room for a couple of nice gold chains, one with a diamond pendant. They each selected a brooch, and then, fully loaded, were ready to go.

They closed the jewellery cases and returned them to the drawer. There were several nice pieces they would have liked to have taken, but bulk and weight had to be considered, and it was quite a long walk home. They did not bother to relock the drawer, concurring with the stable door and horse theory.

'Sam, those burglar alarm wires are rather interesting,' remarked Cosie as they were leaving. 'All the windows are covered, and I noticed that both the front and back doors are wired up.'

'I know. The police will have a real headache trying to figure out how it was done.'

They left as they had entered, and went carefully home, keeping to the shadows. Jess was waiting for them, having woken during the night to find them missing. They padded in, and she emptied their little bags on the table. It was as if she had rubbed Alladin's lamp in that modest room. The precious stones caught and reflected the light as though fire had solidified on the table.

They had their usual hugging and kissing session, and Jess placed the haul in their latest safe - under a loose floorboard beneath her bed. Syd was coming in a few days, and did she have a surprise for him!

As it turned out, she had more than one surprise for him.

Sam went solo the following night to the house of a Mrs. Fanshawe (with an 'e'), whose diamond solitaire ring he had long admired. While taking tea in The Hey Diddle Diddle, she had moaned endlessly about her husband's habit of leaving open the bedroom window, complaining that the draught dried her skin, and the rustle of leaves from a tree whose branches brushed the window sill kept her awake. Sam felt sure she was the kind of woman who would take off her ring before retiring, and put it on her dressing table or bedside cabinet. Such proved to be the case, and it was a very brief night's work to teach her to be more careful in future.

Mrs. Fanshawe's solitaire duly joined the hoard under the floorboard.

Syd was getting on his feet again. He had picked up most of his old contacts, and was losing the pinched, prison look which was so unlike his usual self.

They had a splendid dinner in a nearby restaurant, and Jess asked that they go back to her flat for coffee and brandy, as she had something to discuss with him.

They settled on the sofa with the mellow spirit, and reminisced about Richard and the war.

'You know Jess, I'm just about all right now,' Syd said expansively, puffing on an enormous cigar, and moving Butty to a more comfortable position on his lap. 'If you need any help, you know you only have to say the word.'

'As a matter of fact, I do need help, but perhaps not the kind you think.'

She rose gracefully and disappeared into the bedroom. Syd heard some scraping, woody noises, and in a few moments she returned carrying a canvas bag. She tipped the contents onto the table, and Syd promptly spilled his brandy all over Butty, and put the wrong end of the cigar into his mouth. When he had composed himself, he walked over to examine the glittering treasure laid out for his inspection.

These are the things Richard left you, and you've hung on to them all this time!'

'No, they're not from Richard. They are stolen, but just last week. I don't think you will believe me if I tell you how I got them.'

'Jess, you've gone into the business. Richard taught you and you're out on your own! Oh Christ, love, don't.

You will get caught. Prison is terrible, take my word. Give it up Jess. Make these the last.'

'I give you my word that I did not personally steal them. I can also guarantee that the thieves will never go for trial, and certainly will never be imprisoned. I just want you to handle them for me, and give me the same deal as you gave Richard.'

'Of course I'll look after you, but I won't pretend I like it.'

Syd went to bed that night a baffled and very worried man.

Over the next few months, the team did a job on average every six weeks - always jewels, always the best.

Jess bought a small car, and a method evolved whereby an out-of-town dweller who seemed promising was 'marked' for Jess by a disgusting display from Butty. This involved the subject being jumped on, purred at deliriously, rubbed against, headbutted, and generally being treated as the second coming. In the process of collecting the slobbering Butty, Jess could engage the prospective target in conversation, and find out roughly where she lived (exact address to be determined later from the telephone directory). They would then all pile into the car, and when conditions were favourable, Jess would park a short distance away. The cat-burglars would then go to the house, do the business, and return to the car to be driven home.

On one such occasion, they were visiting the home of one Mrs. Rogers in St. John's Wood, when disaster very nearly overtook them.

Mrs. Rogers had informed her friend Pamela that a safe had recently been installed for their valuables, and the team rather fancied cracking it, an endeavour they had not attempted before. Owing to her poor memory, Mrs. Rogers had found it necessary to enter the combination in her diary, a fact which she also confided to Pamela.

Butty had been lurking under the table during this interesting conversation, and it was the work of a moment to unclasp Mrs. Rogers' handbag, find her small, leather-bound diary, and flip through until he found the required notation. He immediately went to the back room, where Cosie committed the information to his excellent memory.

When next she visited The Hey Diddle Diddle, Jess overheard Mrs. Rogers telling Pamela of the family's planned visit to the Opera that evening. Jess and Sam exchanged a meaningful look, and as the Rogers clan settled down to enjoy Carmen, Raffles' Rivals were deposited at the gate of their house.

Jess parked the car at a pre-determined spot a few streets away, and awaited the successful conclusion of the raid. Should anything untoward happen, she would sound a sharp warning on the car's horn.

The house was a mock-Tudor affair, whose white exterior walls were criss-crossed with timber. There was no cat-flap, and all the reachable windows were securely locked.

'We'll just have to break one of those little panels in the French window,' Sam concluded, although he hated damaging property.

Cosie, being the strongest, dragged a stone from the rockery, and forced it through the glass. Butty, whose thick fur was impenetrable by anything short of a speeding bullet, went in first, clearing away the shards of glass to ensure safe passage for the other two.

Jason was a bulldog. His youth was a long-forgotten memory, and if Butty could accurately be described as fat, Jason could equally accurately be described as gargantuan. He was extremely ugly, and slobbered alarmingly. His major claim to fame as a guard dog was that an intruder would be scared half to death at the very sight of him.

It was this leviathan who confronted Butty as he shook bits of glass from his fur onto the lounge floor. Butty was rooted to the spot in a state of shock as Jason's saliva flowed at the sight of this enemy who had been presented to him on a plate. Cosie was half in and half out of the window pane, and Sam was behind him, not knowing what was going on. Cosie's presence of mind saved the situation. With a mighty heave, he freed himself, and with a quick leap was on the astonished Jason's back, scratching the tender parts beneath his squiggly little tail. The sound galvanised Butty, who fastened his teeth into a roll of fat on the unfortunate dog's side. By this time, Sam was in the room, and sizing up the situation instantly, he ordered his troops to run. They regrouped at the top of the staircase, and Sam rapidly gave his instructions.

'Cosie, go straight to the bedroom and try the safe; close the door behind you. Butty and I will keep the dog occupied.' Jason was lumbering up the stairs, making deep, frightening growling noises, and blocking the downward path with his bulk. Sam and Butty waited until he was within snapping distance, then Sam gave him a smart clout across the nose. Jason yelped, but gallantly pursued his attackers. As soon as the staircase was clear,

Sam and Butty raced to the bottom and sat making insulting noises at Jason, until he started to chase them.

They ran all over the ground floor of the house. First Sam would almost let himself be caught, then Butty would attack from the rear. The poor dog did not know if he was coming or going, and his limited store of energy was fading rapidly.

Finally, Jason's reserves were exhausted. He flopped down on the soft hall carpet, full of a sense of humiliation and failure. It isn't fair, he thought. A bulldog is the very symbol of the indomitable British - firm, fair and aggressive. The cats, wherever it was they came from, didn't stand and fight, didn't play fair, and attacked from the rear when you weren't looking. Jason concluded they must be Russians.

During the mêlée, Cosie was working on the safe. It had a small dial which was able to manipulate with his teeth. As each number was dialed and the tumblers fell into place, Cosie's excitement mounted. When he completed the combination, he sat back and regarded the safe with trepitdation. Would it open? Were there more alarms about? Only one way to find out, he thought, and firmly gripped the handle in his mouth. He pulled downwards, and with agonising slowness the handle began to shift. Bit by bit he worked it down, then inched the heavy door open. It was well worth the effort. A splendid array of jewellery was revealed, together with a considerable sum in cash.

Cosie selected the items they could comfortably carry, and placed them on the bed with the money.

Butty stayed downstairs to keep an eye on the half-dead Jason, while Sam went to the bedroom to see how Cosie was getting on.

'Well done Cosie! We're really top-flight now we've done a safe. We'll pack our pouches, then you can watch the watch-dog and Butty can get loaded. We'll divide the money and carry a wad each in our mouths.'

When the transportation arrangements were completed, they gathered in the lounge, and left via the window-pane. Jason watched them with baleful eyes, but his legs had died, and he could do no more than cry tears of rage and beat his head on the floor with frustration.

Sam, Butty and Cosie rejoined Jess in the car, and they drove home in high spirits.

The local police were completely baffled by the case, one wit concluding that a group of garden gnomes had taken to crime, since people-sized burglars could not have utilised so small an entrance as that provided by the broken pane of glass. The insurance company was sceptical about the whole thing, and met the claim with bad grace and the utmost reluctance.

Of course, not all their expeditions were successful. There were houses where they unable to gain admittance; others were too well protected by alarms, or more than one dog. In the main, however, their schemes went off like clockwork. Jess and Syd prospered mightily, and it was just like the old days.

Butty had become a compulsive delver into handbags and shopping bags. Ladies tended to leave them under the table near their feet while they were eating, and practice had led to expertise. There was not a clasp which could defeat Butty, and as for shopping bags, he could sniff out and devour his favourite delicacies in five seconds flat. It was a particular joy to find the neatly wrapped packages which originated in Harrods' Food

Hall, and he was addicted to their smoked salmon. His method was to carefully unwrap the food and devour it, then refold the paper exactly as it had been before its contents were appropriated by the fastest jaws in England - possibly Europe. This caused great consternation to Harrods' customers, who would arrive home to find empty paper bags; to Harrods, who received many complaints; and to Jess, who could not understand why Butty was becoming so fat.

He was also a hoarder of championship class. Cosie joked that there was a squirrel somewhere in the mists of Butty's ancestry, a fact which also would account for his extravagant tail. Butty took no notice, and collected a truly amazing conglomeration of gloves, lipsticks, combs and nailfiles. He had a repository in the garden shed, and spent hours sorting and re-arranging his treasures. As long as he did not steal anything which could point an accusatory finger at The Hey Diddle Diddle, Sam and Cosie accepted his kleptomania with amused tolerance.

One day, Butty was reclining on the lap of a certain Dr. Frances Webster, a great favourite of his, who could induce him to quiver with pleasure with her knowledgeable stroking and tickling. Dr. Webster was not a wealthy woman, and certainly did not go in for such fripperies as jewellery. They all liked her, and the way she spoke of her cat Balthazar, a Persian of impeccable pedigree, and apparently delightful disposition. They would have liked to meet him.

'I do so sympathise with you Gloria. There is nothing worse than insomnia. You look so exhausted.' Dr. Webster was lunching with her sister, and since there were few other customers, Butty was relaxing, and almost asleep. I think I might be able to help you. Remember when I was working at the American Hospital during the war? There was so little we could do for some of the boys, particularly the burns cases. We did a lot of research on sleeping drugs, and developed a pill that knocks you out in five minutes. There is no uncomfortable whoozy period. You just dissolve two tablets in a hot drink - they are quite tasteless - and you go straight to sleep. I was a bit naughty, and kept some after the war. I have twelve for you in my handbag. They have absolutely no side-effects and are completely safe provided you take no more than two at a time. A few good nights' sleep will at least help to carry you over this bad time with that dreadful husband of yours.'

Butty thought that these tablets could be a useful addition to his stores. Sometime, he thought, they might come in handy. He yawned, stretched, and jumped down from Dr. Webster's lap. Her handbag was on the floor, and clasped shut. This presented no difficulty to Butty, and it was open in a matter of seconds. He pawed through the contents until he found a little bag with the pills inside. He took them from the bag, which he reclasped, and sauntered off to the garden with the bag in his mouth, taking care to keep his head down and his neck fur fluffed up to conceal his prize.

Dr. Webster was very flustered when she discovered her loss, but convinced herself that she had left the pills at home.

'And what on earth are we going to do with sleeping tablets,' Sam enquired when Butty told him of his latest acquisition.

'You never can tell. One day we might need some of my things, and then you and Cosie will see just how clever and far-sighted I really am.'

Sam doubted that Butty's miscellany of bits and pieces would ever see the light of day operationally, but he was used to Butty's quirks, and just grinned good-humouredly.

Lady Josephine Mountbourne was adored by everyone in The Hey Diddle Diddle. She appealed strongly to their sense of the dramatic. Her voice was geared to reach the back row of the stalls, and she was incapable of speaking without illustrating her point with extravagant gestures. Lady Josephine was about fifty-five, tall and straight backed with short fair hair, strands of which seemed to have minds of their own, which refused to occupy their appointed places in her coiffure. She had the habit of running her hands through her hair when excited, which was often, and frequently left The Hey Diddle Diddle looking as if she had been unable to escape the path of a localised tornado. Her favourite garment was a voluminious black cloak which she donned with great flourish, like Kathy preparing to brave the Moors for an assignation with Heathcliffe. Her favourite exclamation was 'Oh my God!' which she would cry whilst attacking her long-suffering hair. Her favourite quantitive adjective was 'thousands' which she used to describe any number larger than two.

This unforgettablc and entertaining client was unique in that she alone found Cosie irrestistable. By this time, he was handsome and imposing, rather than fluffy and pretty like Butty, or impish and amusing like Sam. Cosie was dispensing his strictly limited favours, and keeping half an ear on the chatter between Lady Josephine and her friend The Honourable Mrs Willoughby, when he heard the news about the party.

'Thousands are coming Phyllis. I am sure I shall be quite exhausted at the end of it. Still, one's only son's engagement must be celebrated, and it will be nice to have the house full again. The last big party we had was before the war. Many of those dear guests are dead now, of course. Such a terrible waste. I have to open up thousands of bedrooms for the people from the country. One cannot ask them to leave London in the middle of the night, so there will be thousands of people for breakfast too... Oh my God! I don't know how I shall cope.'

'Josephine stop being dramatic. You know you will cope perfectly well, and it will be wonderful party. You will enjoy yourself enormously, and queen it over everyone disgracefully.' Pyllis Willoughby had been Josephine's friend since they were girls, and was one of the few allowed to voice such candid comments on her extravagant personality.

Because she was such a darling, and so highly placed in their league table of acceptable people, Sam, Butty and Cosie had agreed that her jewellery was sacrosanct. In addition, Lady Josephine did not much care for gold and precious stones. She had a penchant for great silver brooches and necklace designed and made for her by her husband, whose hobby was making jewellery. Each piece was unique, and marked an event in their lives together. The cats did not want to deprive her of these memories. They had given her house the once over when she first came to The Hey Diddle Diddle, and decided that had it been owned by anyone else, they would definitely consider it a viable proposition. It was a little too far away for comfortable transportation of the haul, but within their capabilities.

The party presented the cats with a dilemma. A celebration of such magnitude was an opportunity not to be missed. Guests would be dressed in their finery and displaying their baubles. When they finally went to bed, a variety of desireable items would undoubtedly be carelessly strewn around the various bedrooms.

On the night of Gerald's engagement party, the three uninvited guests waited in the garden until the party was in full swing. A band played in the ballroom, and brightly clad dancers whirled around the floor. Tables struggled to support a sumptious buffet, and champagne flowed in a frothing, bubbly cateract.

The cats' appetities had been sharpened by the long walk to the house, and the wait in the open air. Butty was in an agony of frustration at the sight of so much food just out of his reach, and scanned the room for some that was accessible. At last he spotted a low table just to the side of the open french windows. The table sported smoked salmon, drumsticks and cold cuts. Butty sneaked over to the table and concealed himself beneath the overhanging tablecloth. A fat, gray paw could have been seen appropriating three chicken drumsticks, three slices each of ham and roast beef, and a vast amount of smoked salmon. Once the supplies were saftely under the table, a fat gray shape could have been seen ferrying them out to the garden. Luckily, no one was looking, the impromptu picnic was much enjoyed, and Lady Josephine's catering much complimented.

After their feast, they stationed themselves outside the kitchen door to await developments.

Around one a.m., a reveller who had obvioulsy imbibed far more than was good for him, felt the need of the fresheness of the garden. He also needed its anonimity in which to be sick. He opened the kitchen door shakily, and as he stepped out into the darkness, did not notice three furry shapes glide in behind him. Sam checked that the coast was clear, and they followed him up the back staircase to the first floor, and hid themselves under the bed of what was obviously the master bedroom.

'You see the difference breeding makes,' Butty said appreciatively looking around the room. 'Mrs Abercrombie-Smyth's room is a monument to bad taste in comparison. Lady Josephine's decorations and furnishings are impeccable.'

As always their plan was the essence of simplicity. They would start here with a small item of Lady Josephine's, then gain access to all the other bedrooms on the first floor by way of the little balconies conveniently abutting each French window. The space between balconies was slightly hazardous to cross, the only route being by way of the thick ivy which covered the house. They would leave via the roof of the covered porch, from where it was just a small jump to the ground. They knew they would not be trapped in Lady Josephine's room, since she was something of a fresh-air fiend, and always slept with her windows wide open - winter or summer.

The party was an enormous success, and went on well into the small hours. At last the house settled down, guests went to their rooms, and fell into the heavy sleep of those who have truly enjoyed themselves, and whose stomachs are full of the finest food and drink.

Sam and Cosie woke Butty up, and they packed Lady Josephine's diamond brooch into Sam's pouch. They had heard her say on several occasions that she did not care much for it. They slid silently out of the window onto the balcony, and made the slightly nerve-wracking transfer to its neighbour. No luck there, the window was closed. The next one was open, however, and Butty packed in a lovely matching set of emerald earrings, necklace and brooch. They covered all the bedrooms with open windows. By the time they reached the last one, the strain of crawling across the tangled ivy was enormous, particularly for Butty who had more weight to haul. He cursed evry morsel he had stolen, and vowed to commence a stringent diet the following day. They had a varied collection of earrings, necklaces and bracelets, and several rings, including to Butty's delight, a superb sapphire set in diamonds.

The last bedroom they visited was the one directly over the porch. They were exhausted, and fell rather than jumped onto its roof, and thence to the ground. They passed silently through the bars of the high metal gate, and into the deserted street. On the long trek home they had to pause frequently to rest, and to allow Butty to get his breath back. At last they arrived home, to find Jess waiting for them with warm milk, and dishes of small fish - their favourite.

They flopped down on the sofa, and she unpacked their pouches. Once again the small room was lit by the reflected fire of precious stones and the dull gleam of gold.

'My poor darlings. You must be exhausted. You have carried so much.' She petted them, relaxed them, loved them, and their flagging spirits soon revived. In the short time, the usual celebrations were observed, and the haul stowed safely under the floorboards.

This latest and most successful of their ventures was to have unforseen and serious repercussions. What Lady Josephine had omitted to mention in their hearing was that her brother-in-law was the Assistant Commissioner of Police at Scotland Yard.

CHAPTER NINE
DETECTIVE INSPECTOR RADLEY

Jonathon Radley was the brightest and fastest rising star in the Metropolitan force. He was in his early thirties, tall and dark haired, more like a film star than a copper. His subordinates always referred to him as Radish. It was Detective Inspector Radley's unfortunate lot to be assigned to the spate of jewel robberies which was blighting the crimes solved figures.

He was summoned to the office of the Assistant Commissioner, and told in no uncertain terms that, not only was he expected to apprehend the culprits, but he was expected to do it by yesterday.

'You cannot imagine what it is like to be hounded by my sister-in-law. She telephones at least four times a day to find out if we have made any progress, and will not be satisfied until the thieves have been publicly executed in Hyde Park. I am sure I shall not need to tell you again how anxious I am to see results.' The Assistant Commissioner's voice had acquired a distinct edge, and Radley, who knew something of the baffling robberies, felt much as the members of the Light Brigade must have felt when ordered to ride into the valley of death.

He started by extracating the files on all the unsolved robberies in the area for the past year. The first thing that struck him as odd, was that in many cases, although entry and exit had been achieved successfully, with no evidence that the thieves had been disturbed, many valuable items had been left untouched. Silverware, paintings, porcelain and valuable furs had been ignored. Why? It appeared that the thieves specialised in jewellery, but in may cases, they had not taken all the available pieces. Why? It was a puzzle. Why go to all the trouble of getting in and then leave without taking everything with you?

He decided to revisit the scenes of crimes to see if he could come up with a new angle. His first visit was to Mrs. Abercrombie-Smythe. He was ushered into the Library to await the presence.

'I thought we were finished with all this, were her first words as she swept into the room, giving Radley a look which would have turned the Gorgon to stone. 'You would have caught them by now if you were going to. I really don't k we pay all these taxes. It is just sheer inefficiency. Do you read Miss Christie's books? Poirot would have caught the wretches. It is a pity the police are not as clever.'

Radley admitted that he was not familiar with Miss Chrisitie's mysteries, but promised to remedy the omission.

'What I am trying to do, Mrs. Abercrombie-Smythe, is bring a new eye to bear. They are very cunning, these thieves. They leave no trace, no fingerprints. In many of the robberies, we cannot even be sure how they got in. We need help, I don't mind telling you.'

After grovelling suitably for a while, and ladling on the charm in large dollops, Radley had Mrs. Abercrombie-Smythe captivated, and had to listen to her entire life story from when she was a 'gel' in Hampshire, through days as a Memsahib in India, to the present round of charity work, gossiping with friends and shopping.

'Give me a timetable for a typical week,' he coaxed.

She went to friends' houses, entertained a little at home, sat on the committees of numerous charities, met friends before and after shopping, usually at The Hey Diddle Diddle.

'The what?' Radley interjected at this point in the interminable narrative.

'The Hey Diddle Diddle. You know - the cat and the fiddle, the cow jumped over the moon It's a tea-shop behind Harrods. Very cosy and genteel. Nice for afternoon tea and suchlike. Lots of my friends meet there.'

The Hey Diddle Diddle duly found its way into Radley's notebook, along with reams of other useless information.

He thanked his hostess for her co-operation, and went on to his next call. A Mrs. Fanshawe.

'As you can see, Inspector, it is a complete mystery. I took off my ring before retiring and put it on my bedside cabinet as I always have done. When I awoke in the morning it had gone. Would you like another cup of tea?'

'Please. What puzzles me is that nothing else was taken. You are quite sure of that Mrs. Fanshawe?'

'Yes, I was most thorough. All my other jewellery was in the little safe we have in the study.'

'It seems so odd to go to all the trouble of getting in, and then to take only one ring. Not at all like your usual burglar.'

'Neither I nor my husband heard a single thing.'

'There was no-one else in the house that night? No guests, staff?'

'No, Inspector, just the two of us.'

Radley repeated his speech about searching for a link. Mrs. Fanshawe was a tall, well-dressed woman whose natural habitat appeared to be garden parties, Henley, Ascot and the like, and she related a very similar lifestyle to that of Mrs. Abercrombie-Smythe, including the use of The Hey Diddle Diddle as an unofficial club.

The hairs on the back of Radley's neck were beginning to prickle. He resolved to visit this popular establishment in the very near future.

Radley visited four victims in the following few days, all of whom were regular clients of The Hey Diddle Diddle. Definitely time for a visit he thought.

He had hoped to fit unobtrusively into the background when he visited the teashop, but this was not to be. He was the only male in the establishment, and his dark good looks evinced animated interest from all the ladies. He was embarrassed, and gave his order to the waitress without looking at her. His tea and muffins appeared on his table, and no more that ten minutes later, Mrs. Abercrombie-Smythe flowed in and pounced on him.

'My dear Inspector Radley,' she gushed. 'How absolutely delightful to see you here. 'Jess, do come and meet our guardian of law and order.'

Jess walked over to his table, and he rose to take her proferred hand. Jess's beauty had matured, and the fine angles of her face accentuated her startling violet eyes. Radley was struck not just by her appearance, but also by her air of self-assurance and competence.

At that precise moment, Jess felt anything but self-assured and competent. Her mouth was dry, her heart was thumping, and she felt sure her hand was trembling in his.

Mrs. Abercrombie-Smythe informed Jess that Radley was investigating her recent robbery and those of several of her friends.

'How can I help you Inspector? Shall I surrender the band of desperate fellows I have hidden in the back room? Sam, please don't jump on the Inspector, you will crease his suit.'

'Sam, Butty and Cosie are so much a part of The Hey Diddle Diddle,' trilled Mrs. Abercrombie-Smythe. 'They are like old friends.'

'Sam, Butty and Cosie are my cats,' Jess explained to the Inspector, who was vainly trying to avoid Butty's enthusiastic headbutts. 'They love people, and many of our customers come to be fond of them.' She suppressed a smile at the thought that one of the wanted criminals was sitting on the Inspector's lap, another scrutinising him from floor level, and a third was peering at him from around the kitchen door.

Jess seated herself at Radley's table, and retrieved Sam, placing him on the floor near the Inspector's feet. Sam settled himself, and was soon ostensibly asleep, but in reality, not missing a word. 'Know thine enemy,' he thought. This policeman could cause problems, although he almost certainly would never link The Hey Diddle Diddle's cats with the crimes he was investigating. It would be just too great a jump for his imagination.

Jess and Jonathon talked for about an hour. The subjects they discussed seemed unrelated, but Sam soon realised that a very professional interrogation was being conducted. Radley soon knew most of Jess's life story, excluding Richard, to whom she never referred except when talking with Syd.

'I felt I had to come here. So many of the victims seem to use this place as a kind of ladies,' club. I think I was looking for an easy solution. Perhaps a waitress with a criminal boyfriend, who eavesdropped on conversations and reported titbits to her lover. But there is only you, and I cannot see you as a gangster's moll.'

'I am very glad to hear that,' Jess commented drily. 'I am just a humble, law-abiding teashop proprietress, struggling to make ends meet.'

Just as Radley was about to leave the teashop, Lady Josephine burst upon the scene, charging through the door with all the impact of a No. 9 bus. She paused dramatically just inside, swirling the left side of her black cloak over her right shoulder, and peering myopically around the room.

'Where is he,' she demanded of the startled customers. 'Where is Radley?'

'I am Inspector Radley,' Jonathon said, walking towards her with his hand extended. 'Might you be Lady Josephine Mountbourne,' From the Assistant Commissioner's description of his sister-in-law, she could not be anyone else.

'Oh my God! What is the man doing here? Why are you not out catching these wretched burglars, instead of wasting time drinking tea? There must be thousands of despicable people you could be investigating. Your office told me you were here. I simply could not believe it, and had to come and see for myself. You are supposed to be a detective, young man. Go off and detect!' Lady Josephine was centre stage, and enjoying herself immensely.

As Radley was the only male present, every eye in the room swivelled expectantly towards him.

'That is precisely what I am doing Lady Josephine,' he retorted. 'Good-day to you madam.' And he was gone, having denied Lady Josephine the pleasure of a public harangue.

Jonathon had enjoyed talking to Jess, and eliminating her from his enquiries. Vicars' daughters from Sussex just did not turn out to be burglars. Vicars' daughters' cats did, on very rare occasions, but Radley had no way of knowing that.

Charmed as he was by Jess, the coincidence of all his victims being customers of The Hey Diddle Diddle kept niggling at him. Was he clutching at straws? These women had very similar lifestyles, was it so unlikely that they should meet in a genteel teashop near to Harrods?

Radley sighed, and returned to his office. He spent another two hours poring over his files and notes, but no great intuitive flashes came. Perhaps I should study Miss Christie's books, he thought ruefully. Maybe I will get some inspiration.

That evening, Jess and the cats were comfortably settled on the sofa. Jess was enjoying an after-dinner brandy, Sam was engrossed in a newspaper account of a recent murder, Cosie was intermittently lapping a bowl of brown ale, and Butty had gone to sleep cuddling a half-eaten bar of chocolate.

'I think we had better go to ground for a while,' Jess said to them. 'I don't like that policeman poking about The Hey Diddle Diddle. The chance of him coming up with the right answer is infinitesimal, but I think it best that we be careful. I'll burn your pouches, and that really is all the evidence there is. I can soon make new ones when things cool down a bit.' Sam stretched and nibbled her chin, indicating he was in perfect agreement with her decision, and Cosie rubbed himself against her legs, purring his concurrence. Butty would go along with the decision of the majority.

Jess telephoned Syd, and they arranged to meet at Victoria Station the following evening for the transferrence of the proceeds of Lady Josephine's party.

'This lot's worth a bloody fortune Jess,' Syd gloated, having surreptitiously poked around the contents of the bag as they walked around. He listened attentively as Jess recounted the details of Jonathon Radley's visit.

'I've never come across him myself, but I've heard a fair bit about him from my villains. He is very sharp. Jess, you have got to tell me who is doing the jobs.' It was if he thought that catching her off-guard would lead her into revealing the identiy of the thief who, he was pretty sure, was Jess herself.

'I was never going to tell you, because I know you will not believe me, but on my word of honour what I am going to tell you is the truth.....'

It all tumbled out, right from the first £400 to the origin of the latest haul.

'The cats? Sam, Butty and Cosie? You're damn right I don't believe you! I never heard of anything so ridiculous.' Syd stared at her incredulously.

'Whether you believe it or not, it happens to be true. Don't ask me to explain it, because I can't. But that does not make it any less true. Whatever you believe, we have decided to go to earth for a while. We are not doing any more jobs until Radley has finished with us. I'll keep in touch by 'phone and let you know how we get on.'

'Please be careful Jess. Remember Radley is a copper first, second and third. If he gets the slightest suspicion of you, he'll keep worrying away like a terrier until he nabs you. I'll put the money from this little lot into your bank accounts as usual. I'll forget the silliness about the cats. Real cat-burglars indeed! Take care my favourite lady.' He kissed her on the forehead, and they walked their separate ways.

Radley next appeared at The Hey Diddle Diddle the following Sunday afternoon.

'I am sorry to disturb you on your day off,' he apologised when Jess opened the door to him. 'I would like to ask you a few questions about one of your customers if it is convenient.'

'Of course, Inspector. Please come in and have some tea.'

Jess led him through the deserted teashop and up the stairs to the compact little apartment. Sam, Butty and Cosie were asleep in a disorderly pile on the sofa in the comfortable living room. Jess woke them and shoo-ed them off so she and the Inspector could sit and talk in comfort. She bustled about making tea and a snack in the adjoining kitchen. Radley took the opportunity to prowl around the room, looking for he knew not what. An inspection of her private quarters was, in fact, the purpose of his visit. Try as he might, he could not shake off the feeling that The Hey Diddle Diddle was involved in the robberies somehow. Sam watched his every move intently.

'Now, how can I help you?' Jess asked when they were settled.

'Lady Josephine Mountbourne held a big party last week-end, and had uninvited guests. It looks as though the gang who have been giving us so much trouble recently were responsible. They completely baffle us, and this robbery is no exception. Just like all the others, we cannot figure out how they got in and out; they left plenty of valuable silver and furs; nobody saw or heard anything.' He sipped his tea reflectively, and helped himself to a sandwich. 'Did you know of Lady Josephine's party?' he asked suddenly.

'I do not know my customers as intimately as you appear to think Inspector,' Jess replied somewhat frostily. 'Most of them would consider a teashop proprietress far too inferior in the social pecking order to be included in their gatherings have time to sit gossiping with my customers. I cannot recall Lady Josephine mentioning a party. Perhaps you should ask her if she told me about it.'

'I am sorry to offend you, but I have to ask these questions in order to eliminate you from my enquiries. You see the strange thing is that all the victims use The Hey Diddle Diddle.'

'I don't find that overly strange. Surely it must be obvious that most ladies of means prefer to shop at Harrods, and since we are so close, is it so unlikely that they should take their tea or lunch here when they have finished? It is also a very convenient place for them to meet their friends. You may not have noticed, but Pubs do not generally encourage ladies without their male escorts. This is one of the reasons why I considered that a teashop in this location would be a viable business proposition. Where would you have them meet, Inspector? Outside the ladies' lavatory in the Underground station?'

Jess had voiced Radley's own reason for wanting to forget The Hey Diddle Diddle, and he felt rather foolish.

'Could you please tell me where you were on the evening of the Saturday before last?'

'Certainly.' The voice had acquired sharp tones he had not noticed before. 'I was here listening to the radio. My only companions were Sam, Butty and Cosie, but I am afraid I cannot ask them to confirm my alibi. Unless, of course, you are able to communicate with cats.'

Jess rose and began to clear away the crockery.

'If there is nothing else I really would like to terminate this interview.' She was all outraged dignity, but Radley was a very shrewd policeman, who had learned to trust his instincts. He knew there was something wrong somewhere, although he simply could not picture her in the role of cat-burglar. Perthaps she had trained the cats to be thieves! He laughed inwardly at this ridiculous flight of fancy, and looked over at Sam, Butty and Cosie who were lying on the rug. Butty was fast asleep, but Sam and Cosie were staring at him, and Radley thought, with a jolt, that there was something very like amusement in their eyes!

Jess caught his look, and decided he should be got rid of without delay.

'Inspector?'

'Oh, I am sorry. No there is nothing else. Thank you for your co-operation. I hope we can meet again soon.' He took his leave in a slightly preoccupied manner, and Jess felt little tingles of apprehension prickling her spine.

When she had seen him out, Jess poured herself a stiff drink and sat sipping it thoughtfully. Sam jumped on her lap immediately, sensing her concern. Cosie sat beside her, resting his head on her knee. She stroked Sam's lustrous black fur, and talked seriously to them.

'There is nothing to link us to the robberies. The only way they can get to us is if they catch Syd selling it, and he tells them. We all know that Syd would never betray us, so we just have to keep our nerve and sit it out. We have no stolen property here, and they can't ask me awkward questions about my money, because the bank accounts are all in false names. Radley would really have to catch you on site to crack the case. We will be all right little ones, as long as we don't do anything silly.' Sam was of the same mind. He had great respect for Radley, but could not image how he could get anything to go on.

Radley had returned home with his brain in turmoil. Having once mentally voiced the concept of genuine cat-burglars, he could not get it out of his head. The mere fact that the idea was absurd did not make it go away. After all, it was absurd that the gang could get in and out of houses bristling with alarms with apparent ease, and leave no trace of their passing. And it did answer the biggest outstanding question he had - namely why so many items of value had been left behind. If you happened to be less than a foot high, and something like two feet from nose to tail, you were strictly limited in what you could carry! How was it done, he puzzled. Some sort of bag attached to their collars. Yes, that was it. They all wore collars. The more he thought about it, the more it made sense. Jess must do the leg-work listening to the women gossiping at The Hey Diddle Diddle, transport the cats to the chosen victim's house, and bring them home afterwards. He did not credit Sam, Butty and Cosie with the intelligence gathering, nor the fact that locally, they travelled under their own steam. He did not know about the out-of-town robberies. They were handled by different Forces, and details had not filtered back to him. He was, therefore, ignorant of the full extent of their nefarious activities.

That night, when Radley tried to accept a crazy idea which was in fact the truth, Jess went to bed and cried herself to sleep. She longed for the comfort of Richard's arms. She craved the indulgence of weakness, and abdication from responsibility. She wanted to be soothed, to be a woman, to be told it would be all right. She wanted Richard's strength.

Jess woke in the morning feeling better for a good cry, and decided that the chances of Radley arresting them were virtually nil. Radley woke in the morning, and went over what he had so far.

Several families belonging to the same social group had been burgled. The ladies of those families all frequented a teashop owned by a vicar's daughter of apparently impeccable character. He, the investigating officer, had a hare-brained idea that the teashop owner had somehow trained her three cats to be daring and efficient burglars. He spent hours searching for a scheme to get proof of his suspicions. Everything he thought of sounded ludicrous. He pictured himself standing in front of the Assistant Commissioner, reporting that he suspected the existence of three real cat-burglars, and that he proposed to have their house watched.

'Oh indeed Radley,' he could hear the old man say, as he twirled his luxuriant handlebar moustache, 'and do you think these criminals will be dangerous if cornered? Should we, perhaps, turn the whole thing over to the police dogs?'

CHAPTER TEN
THE BIG JOB

Sam, Cosie and Butty were bored. There was nothing in the world like being a cat-burglar, and they missed the clandestine excitement of their nefarious activities. They tried other pastimes. Sam and Cosie played a fair game of Chess, they quite enjoyed Monopoly with its crisp money, and they tried to teach Butty to play Poker. He was, however, a very emotional cat, and went into raptures whenever he was dealt anything higher than a pair.

Every few days Radley would drop in for a 'chat'. He haunted them. Jess was convinced that he had solved the puzzle, and knew about her unorthodox gang. He always took great interest in the trio, and enquired as to their characters and proclivities. Although Jess was always polite to him, his visits were a strain. Butty became sick of the sight of Radley, and resolved to discourage him. First he tried depositing large quantities of his luxuriant gray fur all over Radley's dark trousers, then a couple of long deep scratches on his hands. In desperation, he sidled under Radley's table and peed all over his shoes, which earned him a stern public ticking off from Jess in the teashop, and a cuddle and hysterical amusement in the privacy of the back room. Sam always sat a few feet away from Radley, glowering at him with ill-concealed hatred, and Cosie watched him like a hawk from behind the back door.

Jess spent many hours pondering their future. The proceeds of their robberies were considerable, and Syd had banked half of her share under false names all over London. This was her security - totally safe, clean money. Long ago, she and Syd had decided to become 'backers,' of other, human criminals. Many cleverly planned raids needed capital to buy equipment, getaway cars, and the purchase of a guard's loss of memory or carelessness in locking up. The investment return was a percentage of the proceeds. Syd was known to a strictly limited circle amongst the anonymous cream of the criminal fraternity as a reliable money-man, who would put up the money, handle the goods, and refrain from shopping you afterwards for the insurance reward. In this way, Jess's money had grown far quicker than by more conventional methods of investment, and she was now a moderately wealthy woman. She had used this part of her capital to invest in Syd's other passion - antiques and paintings. Syd had assembled a fine collection for her, which reposed snugly and anonymously in a warehouse in Sussex.

Syd had also branched out to France. Several trips had resulted in the acquisition of many fine pieces at good prices in the wake of the post-war economic chaos. They jointly owned a splendid collection lodged quietly in

Cannes. Jess had visited the South of France the previous spring, and had been enchanted.

One evening in early December, Jess's thoughts were on a recent conversation with Syd. Syd was worried about the Radley situation and its effect on Jess.

'Let's face it love, he's getting to you. You are nervy and edgy, and that is no way to be successful criminal. One of these days he'll wear you down, and you'll want to confess just to get him off your back. I have a suggestion. I don't want to be a villain all my life, and I'm sure you don't either. I think we should quit while we are ahead. Besides, those burglars of yours are not going to be able to carry on forever.' Syd had finally accepted that their prosperity rested upon the efforts of four-legged friends rather than the two-legged variety.

'Remember how you loved the South of France?' he continued. 'Well, what I think we should do is go into the antique business full-time - me in England, and you in France. The only people with any money these days are the Yanks, and they'll pay anything for a bit of European culture in their homes. I made some good contacts when their Army was here, and we could do a tie-up between Europe and the States. Perhaps even get a shop in New York eventually. It could be the answer for both of us. Have a think about it.'

Jess had been thinking of very little else. It was a wonderful opportunity to change the direction of her life. Her French was reasonable, and would improve rapidly with use. She looked fondly at the cats, whose skill and daring had been the means by which she had built a life for herself after Richard's death. Sometimes she had been lonely, but she felt that she was one of the few whose lives had been touched by exceptional happiness -

however briefly - and that she would rather cherish her memories than embark on a search for what would inevitably be a settlement, a second-best.

Butty was asleep, stretched out with his head in the grate, his tail twitching spasmodically as he dreamed of the world's largest smoked salmon being presented to him whole. Cosie was curled up in his favourite armchair, and Sam was on her lap.

'I want to talk to you three.' Jess deposited Sam on the rug, woke Butty and Cosie, and sat down among them in front of the fire.

'You all know that we have been very lucky so far with the way things have turned out. We have been incredibly successful criminals.' The cats visibly swelled with pride, and Butty gave Jess's knees a swaggering headbutt. 'You also know that our investments in other enterprises - both legal and illegal - have generated a lot of money. However, we have come to a crossroads, my darlings. Radley's interest in us makes it essential that we sit down and take stock of what we are going to do next, and where we are going to do it. We have taken our chances, and fortunately we have been lucky. One thing we must never forget, though, is that if Radley gets us, then he'll plug along doggedly until he gets Syd too.'

They were concentrating hard now, and Sam had a momentary flash of deja vu to the time she had announced their departure from Chelsea.

'What Syd has suggested, and having thought about it, I am in agreement, is that we both go legitimately into the antiques business. Syd would run the English end, and we... ' she hesitated slightly and looked into their faces, whose expressions ranged from total incomprehension from Butty, through Cosie's alert curiosity, to Sam's grave attention '... would move to the South of France and handle the French and European end. We would buy a house and live in France, Cannes I think. It is very beautiful, and I know we will all be happy there. Basically, what it means is, an end to our criminal activities. We're going straight!'

The cats looked at each other, then at Jess. What would they do with themselves? No raids to plan; no excitement. Retirement! They trooped off to the kitchen for a private conference.

'Well, that was a bombshell!' Cosie observed, picking at a piece of meat that Butty had missed from supper.

'They speak a different language, we won't be able to talk to the females,' Butty wailed.

'Isn't it always warm there Sam? Isn't the food all fancy,' Cosie was analysing the probable changes they would face.

'I don't know any more about it than you two,' Sam hated to admit it. 'We all read the books Jess brought back with her, and the photographs were lovely. I can't see how the food can be much different from ours. After all, a French fish can't be much different from an English fish, or a French cow or sheep much different from an English cow or sheep. I think it's just the way they cook things. They seem to use lots of something called garlic, and I remember hearing Syd say it makes your breath smell. Jess won't expect us to eat that sort of muck. I think they eat snails a lot, and I have tried one or two in the garden. They were quite nice.'

'Well, I suppose it had to happen sooner or later.' Cosie and Butty had celebrated their birthday recently, and Cosie was becoming conscious of his age. 'We are none of us getting any younger, and I must admit that climbing around in that ivy at Lady Josephine's took it out of me. But I must say I'm not sure if I am ready to spend my days lazing in the sun just yet.'

'At least we can spend our nights having fun.' Butty had always been romantic. 'It always says in the films that Frenchwomen are fantastic. If they are, then their female cats must be too. Frenchwomen always seem to be described as 'women of the world'. I'm not sure what it means, but the phrase always seems to make the men lick their lips and nod their heads.'

The practical Cosie had the last word.

'It doesn't really matter if we like it or not. It's going to happen. But I for one am not looking forward to crossing Channel. I am sure I shall suffer dreadfully from seasickness.'

'I agree,' said Sam dreamily. 'But wouldn't it be nice to pull one last job. A big one. A kind of farewell from us to Radley.'

The 'big job' Sam longed for was dangled in front of them the very next day.

They had eaten their breakfast, dug up a few plants in the garden next door, and were having a well-earned rest in front of the fire. Jess had left the radio on, and the perfect tones of the BBC Newsreader were imparting information which made them all sit up and take notice.

'Harrods have announced a great exhibition of priceless jewellery as part of their Christmas celebrations, commencing next Monday. The jewels will be displayed on a giant Christmas tree, and will be guarded day and night. The main features are a tiara made by Fabergé for the last Czarina of Russia, which includes the greatest of all the Romanov diamonds; two Fabergé necklaces, one of emeralds and one of sapphires, made for the Archduchesses Sophie and Anastasia; a unique diamond bracelet loaned by the Vanderbilt family; a pair of emerald pendant earrings given by Napoleon to the Empress Josephine, and a diamond ring which was worn by Mrs. Aston on the night the Titanic sank. Also included are items of great interest loaned by de Beers, and several of the major houses in Hatton Garden.

'The Prime Minister in a speech to the House of Commons, said that in his view... '

The Prime Minister's view was of no interest to them whatsoever.

'I wonder if there is anything in the paper. Have a look Butty.' Sam was already at the planning stage. They were in and out of Harrods all the time. It was their favourite shop, and they knew all its corridors, back staircases, and nooks and crannies like the backs of their paws. Butty pulled the Daily Express onto the floor, and Page four was devoted to the exhibition.

There was an artist's impression of the jewellery hall, showing the various display cases and small exhibits, and a huge Christmas tree right in the middle, with the jewels taking the place of lametia and glass balls. The Express printed a full list of the exhibition's contents, and it was obvious, even to Butty, that they would need to be selective.

What interested Sam most was a small exhibit in the corner of the Hall, at the side of one of the doors. It featured ancient artefacts and jewellery from Egypt. The display was mounted on representations of the Egyptian cat-God - Anubis. There were statues both large and small, adorned with fine pendants, ear-drops and head-dresses, worked mostly in lapis lazuli.

The Express went on to say that the security was enormous and impregnable. Three men would be stationed by the tree at all times, and would be locked in at night. There would be guards outside every door, and there were, of course, other safeguards which Harrods would not make public.

'Right,' Sam said briskly. 'The first thing is to decide what we are going for.'

'Don't you think that's a bit premature,' Cosie liked a logical progression in their planning.

'No. What we have to carry is an important factor. Don't forget we do not have our pouches any more. The Romanov stuff of course. The tiara and necklaces can go round our middles. The Vanderbilt bracelet can go round my neck. Napoleon's present can be clipped to our collars, along with any other earrings we take a fancy to. We can each carry a ring in our mouths, and if we have any more room, we can take our pick of what is left.'

'What about that tiara with the Star of Ceylon sapphire,' Butty as always was mesmerised by sapphires.

'Good heavens no! That is on loan from Queen Elizabeth herself. That would be treason, and absolutely disloyal.' Cosie was very patriotic. 'You will just have to be content with the Romanov sapphires.'

'Let's not go too mad,' Sam said drily. 'Any single item would keep us quite nicely for about a hundred years. We must not let greed be our downfall. It says here they are erecting the tree the night after tomorrow. I think I'll join them. We'll all pop down there tomorrow night for a look round, and I'll check out a few ideas I have. In the meantime, Butty, you can rake our your sleeping pills. I apologise profusely. It seems that one of your treasures at least will come in handy.'

Sam sat in front of Butty and Cosie, and stretched himself as much as he could. He sucked in his cheeks and slitted his eyes.

'Now, tell me. Do you think I look Egyptian?'

'You could probably pass at a quick glance, and with my white darkened down, I might just get away with it,' Cosie mused, guessing Sam's thinking. 'Butty, though, looks about as Egyptian as a sausage.'

'Yes, he is a problem. We'll work it out somehow. Something will turn up.'

Late the following afternoon, three unusual Christmas shoppers crept into the store's delivery bay, and concealed themselves in an empty crate.

Eventually, the customers departed, and the store was put to bed for the night.

'We'll take care of business first,' Sam said 'then we can have a look at what's going to be in people's Christmas stockings this year.'

They approached the Jewellery Hall by way of a service staircase, and were desperately disappointed to find its heavy doors locked.

'Well! The best-laid plans of cats and men! You'll have to get in tomorrow while the store's still open so you're not locked out while they are erecting the tree. We'll have to settle for the store tour for now.' Cosie had been looking forward to a browse in Harrods' excellent Book Department.

'Let's have a look at the toys first,' Butty suggested enthusiastically. 'They're always terrific.'

They were indeed terrific. The centre of the Toy Department was given over to a vast train set, with rolling green countryside, perfect little stations, tunnels, trains, and yards of track. The whole thing was operated from two control panels, with little levers for the lights, points and wagons.

They located the master power switch, and Butty and Cosie realised lifetime ambitions to be train drivers. They spent a hysterical hour racing the trains, Butty managing to engineer only one head-on collision.

Meanwhile, Sam wandered off for a game with the armies of toy soldiers, miniature cannon and charging cavalry. Having deployed his battalions, he spent a satisfying time working out how Napoleon could have won at Waterloo.

The diversions continued with a challenge match on a child-sized pinball machine. They dragged over a chair from the dolls' tea-party, and operated the spring with their mouths. Butty proved to be unbeatable, a fact which Cosie attributed to his having munched his way through mountains of food over the years, which had strengthened his jaws.

Let's go straight to the Food Hall now. I'm starving.' Butty hadn't eaten for several hours, and considered himself to be in the first stages of malnutrition.

'Everything will be locked away in a cold room,' Sam chuckled. 'You have absolutely no chance of gorging yourself.'

'You just never know. There might be all manner of goodies just covered with a cloth.'

In the event, Butty was not disappointed. A long glass cabinet with sliding doors was filled with a Butty wonderland of kippers, smoked mackeral, trout and eels. The focus of the display was a huge smoked salmon decorated with caviar and lemons.

Butty drooled with anticipatory greed as he jumped on top of the cabinet, and slid the door open with a trembling paw. As an appetizer, he selected a couple of nice, fat trout, which they shared. Sam and Cosie finished off with a bite or two of salmon, and a mouthful of caviar, which Butty assured them was Beluga. Butty somehow twisted himself into the cabinet, and happily began to decimate the salmon. He felt it was Christmas already.

Cosie made his way to the Book department, and was delighted to find an omnibus edition of Raymond Chandler, his favourite author, on a convenient counter. He settled down to a session with Sam Spade - well pleased with his world.

Sam mooched about the store, pausing to examine items of interest, then set about the serious business of checking the feasibility of his plan.

Eventually, they met up in the Delivery Bay to sleep the night away until the doors were opened, and another day began.

On arrival home, Jess scolded them for their long absence, an indignity they bore with fortitude.

Harrods, on discovering the wreckage in the smoked fish cabinet, reached the conclusion that there must be rodents in the store somewhere, and resolved to purchase a cat to cope with the problem.

Late that afternoon, Sam took a slow stroll down to Harrods. He entered the store via the Delivery Bay. Everyone was busy, and he kept to the shadow. He went to the Jewellery Hall by their little-frequented backstairs route, encountering no-one on the way. The Hall was thronged with Christmas gift buyers, and nobody noticed a small black cat ascend the Egyptian display platform, and metamorphasize into just another Anubis.

Soon it became time for the great store to disgorge its customers and become the charge of the small army of functionaries who cleaned it, restocked it, and finally, guarded it.

Sam watched with great interest the behind-the scenes activity which was the stores' lifeblood.

He had a very nasty moment when Gertie and Glad, the charladies responsible for the pristine cleanliness of the Jewellery Hall stood in front of the Egyptian exhibit. Glad was a generously built lady, who towered over the diminutive Gertie like a splendid English oak giving shelter to a sapling beneath its branches.

'You know, Gert, those cats give me the creeps,' Glad observed to her feather-duster wielding cohort. 'It's something in the eyes. They look like they're following you wherever you go. Not like our English cats at all. Now you take my Whiskers - great soppy thing he is. You couldn't picture him looking all sinister and guarding somebody's tomb. They must have different cats in Egypt. Look at that little black one at the back. Fair gives me the wobblies he does. Right evil those eyes are.'

The little black one under scrutiny, who was trying desperately not to move a muscle, or to breathe, was feeling anything but evil. His ears were twitchy, and he desperately wanted a stretch and a pee.

Finally, with a flick of the dusters here and there, Glad and Gertie moved on, and Sam relaxed.

Soon the service people departed, and the security people arrived.

An enormous Christmas tree, broad rather than tall, was wheeled in and erected in the very centre of the Hall, right in front of Sam's grandstand seat.

The jewels were brought in by a team of six security guards, and lay in their open cases flashing their arrogant brilliance. Sam forgot his discomfort, and gazed entranced as treasure followed treasure. Lastly, the Romanov tiara and necklaces were revealed in all their regal splendour. Even the experienced jewellery men gasped at their magnificence. Sam imagined them bedecking beautiful women dancing in the opulent palaces of Moscow and St. Petersburg, and wondered as he often did at the strange affairs of humans, which had brought these same women to their hideous, sordid deaths at Ekaterinburg. He shook himself slightly to break the reverie, and slowly a warm glow crept over him. This robbery would be a fitting end to their careers, and put them alongside the great jewel thieves of history, none of whom would have looked down on this haul.

The display team worked steadily, and soon the tree was a unique thing of great beauty - a work of art.

Lights were concealed in the thick branches and trained to highlight the myriad colours of diamonds, rubies, sapphires, emeralds and pearls. The Romanov tiara crowned the tree, its diamond the star.

'We are all finished now,' the head display artist said, walking around the tree and gazing critically at the handiwork of his team. 'I'll just tweak this necklace a little... ah, yes, that's it. Just right.' The display team departed, and the Head of Security now took charge.

Mr. Williams was a portly, bustling gentleman, who exuded an air of great competence and efficiency. He strolled around the tree thoughtfully, followed by the respectful gazes of his assistants, and Sam's undivided attention.

'What we have already decided will do nicely. During the day, Roberts and Wilson will be in uniform on opposite sides of the tree. There will be six men and three women in plain clothes mingling with the customers. When the store closes, a search of the Hall will be made, to ensure that no-one is hiding inside, Waterson, Calder and Brown will be locked inside the Hall for the night, and two men will be stationed outside each door. It would take a bloody Houdini to get in and out of that little trap, but just in case, Mr. Jordan here is going to put a little pattern of buttons on the floor, and if anyone treads on them,all hell will break loose. They will go under the carpet, and no-one will know they are there. Any questions?'

'What about our natural functions, Sir?' During the night I mean.' Calder obviously felt embarrassed by the word 'lavatory,' and used substitutes wherever possible.

'We are getting a sort of commode thing brought in. We couldn't have you all busting a gut could we? You would not be much use if you couldn't collar a villain because you were trying to hold in your water.' Williams liked his little joke.

'Will we have anything to make a cup of tea? Can't go all night without wetting the old whistle.' Waterson was the Music Hall Englishman who could virtually colonise the world, sail around it in scruffy little ships, and perform feats of heroic proportions - as long as he had his cup of tea.

'A small spirit stove is coming up from the Camping Department. There will even be a little table and a chair each. It won't be a comfortable chair, mind, and if anyone falls asleep, he'll wish he had never been born. Anything else?'

A general shaking of heads indicated that everyone was happy with the arrangements. The commode, table and chairs duly arrived, and the only remaining task was for Mr. Jordan to install his buttons and alarm bells. Mr. Jordan was a methodical fellow, and the buttons were laid in a zig-zag pattern radiating from directly beneath the lowest branches, to a distance of about three feet from the end of the longest branch. Wires connected them to the alarm box concealed in the tree's container, a vast silver tub, which Sam thought a little ostentatious.

'Any problems, lads, just hit one of those buttons, and the noise will bring the 7th Cavalry galloping to the rescue.'

Sam had already decided on his route up the tree, and had only to fix in his mind the positions of those buttons on the approach. He had to suppress a little giggle. They had covered everything so well, but had not booby-trapped the tree itself. They probably thought it impossible that anyone would be able to get near enough to touch it.

At last, everyone but Waterson, Calder and Brown departed for home. The doors were locked, two men taking up position outside each one, and the stalwart trio settled down to the first night of their vigil.

Sam was aching from staying in one position for so long. He eased each leg in turn, and took his mind off his discomfort by finalising his plans. The tree's branches were easily thick enough for a small cat to use a step-ladder to the items he had marked as their targets.

The biggest problem was camouflaging Butty. The Ancient Egyptians had not gone in for depicting their cat-god with long gray fur and a flattish face. Cosie could be blackened with coal dust, and pass quite well. Butty, however, was a problem. Butty usually was, he thought with resigned affection.

The security trio spent a while familiarising itself with its empire. Waterson and Brown spent some time in front of the Egyptian exhibit.

'Funny lot them Egyptians when you think on,' Waterson said in his ponderous way. 'Fancy worshipping a bunch of frigging cats. You wouldn't think a mob who could build the pyramids and such could set such store by a bunch of tabbies. You can see by just looking at a few in our street that any cat is as thick as two short lance-corporals.'

This little aside swept away any slight feelings of concern Sam had entertained for the guards. They would never know, but 'thick,' cats would achieve what the sophisticated cream of London's human underworld would never even attempt - beat Harrods, and the best security system men could engineer.

All through that Saturday night, Sam observed the guards. He watched them brew their tea at midnight, and guessed this would probably be a regular timing. He watched them perform their 'natural functions', and longed to relieve his own swollen and aching bladder. He listened to their chatter about their wives and families and their humdrum lives, and concluded that his own existence was infinitely preferable. he contrasted their time-governed ways with the joy of roaming the darkened, empty streets - free as air. He fought hand-to-hand with his enemies; loved his many lady friends. There was his love for Jess; the abandoned happiness of rolling in the earth, and feeling the sun on his fur or the rain under his paws; the excitement of a robbery and his camaraderie with Butty and Cosie.

His life was very good. It had joy, and the occasional sorrow, love and laughter. Even his exasperation when Butty was particularly silly, or Cosie was particularly stuffy, was a thing to treasure. It provided his life with light and shade, like the components of a great painting. He recognised that a part of that life would end with this robbery. They would move to France, and start again. There would be no need for Jess to work in the antique business, but she probably would anyway. She did not like to be idle. Perhaps she would meet someone to fill the aching space left by Richard. Perhaps they would all love again, and kittens would be brought home to eventually take their places. Cats did not live as long as humans, and they had decided long ago that replacements would have to be trained so that Jess would be looked after. Sam had a hope that eventually he would bring his son to Jess. His ultimate gift. Black as the night like himself, but with a heart as great and bright as the sun.

The night passed slowly. The guards produced a pack of cards, and sat in a manner which screened Sam from them. He cautiously moved position, and risked a walk around the small dias on which the Egyptian exhibition was mounted. He was no nearer solving the problem of incorporating Butty into the display, until he investigated an enormous model of a coiled cobra, with its head erect, hood flared, and serpent's forked tongue extended. The coils formed a hollow circle. Butty could just curl up inside and go to sleep until the great moment arrived. Everything was working out just beautifully. He went back to his place, and watched for the rest of the night. Nothing happened. There were no unscheduled visits or telephone calls; the guards did nothing but guard.

Promptly at eight o'clock, with a clanking of keys, the day-shift took over. Sam passed unnoticed out of the door, while the two groups exchanged gossip.

He made his way wearily down to the dark cavern of the deserted Delivery Bay, relieved himself on a pile of oily rags, and unearthed his breakfast, which he had squirreled away before his vigil began. He jumped through the open window of one of the delivery vans, curled up on the driver's seat, and sank into the deep sleep of those whose problems have been resolved, and on whom the gods smile.

Sam awoke at about 4.00 p.m. He felt refreshed and relaxed, and well able to complete the rest of his mission.

Cut into the huge double doors of the Delivery Bay was a very small gate to allow passage in and out without the performance of opening the whole exit. It was heavily chained and padlocked, both inside and out. The gate was constructed of vertical wooden slats joined on all sides to horizontal bracing slats. Many years of slamming had made the bottom horizontal slat a little loose. Three nails held it in place, of which two protruded from the wood. It was a small matter for Sam's strong jaws to remove the loose nails and carefully lay them on the ground. The third, and bottom nail, was more stubborn, but now Sam could get a paw behind the slat, and he patiently worked away until it joined the other two on the ground.

The slat was held quite securely in place, but could be opened just wide enough to allow for the passage of a small body - a small body wearing a fortune in jewels. He did a test run in and out, and then carefully replaced the nails, covering the heads with a little mud from the tyres of one of the delivery vans to keep them loosely in place.

For his final task, he first had to re-visit the Toy Department. On the way, he had a wander around the Pet Department. He was not in favour of things like coats and jewelled collars for cats and dogs, and felt sorry for animals who had to let their people make them look silly. He then had a vision of Butty festooned with the Romanov sapphires, and rolled around on the floor with glee.

He wasted no time in the Toy Department, but went straight for what he wanted - plasticine. He grasped two packets in his mouth, and went off to complete his preparations.

It was Monday morning. A cold, crisp, bright English December morning. The delivery men loaded their vans, taking Christmas purchases to the fortunate all over the country. Sam stole out unnoticed amongst the bustle, and made his way home.

'Oh Sam! My Sammy!' Jess scooped him up in her arms and covered him with kisses. 'Where have you been? I've been demented. I looked everywhere for you. I thought you were ill or dead, or hurt by a car. You must be starved, and you are so cold.' She put him in an armchair, wrapped in one of her cardigans, an indignity which Sam endured with tolerant stoicism, and rushed of to prepare food and warm milk.

Butty and Cosie were unconcernedly stretched out on the rug.

'You will never guess what has happened Sam,' Butty joined him in the armchair. 'After you left on Saturday, Radley came in for tea. He steered clear of me, of course, but I did manage to get quite a nice bite on the ankle. Anyway Jess told him we were leaving for France, and he said they must have a farewell dinner. Quite insistent he was. Jess told us later she thought it would be quite a joke to accept, and he is picking her up tomorrow at seven o'clock.'

'That is marvellous. She will have completely watertight alibi for the whole evening.' Sam had worried that Radley would give Jess a bad time after the robbery, but this dinner engagement would make it much more difficult for him.

'Did everything go well in the store,' Cosie asked.

'Absolutely as planned. There is even a good hiding place for Butty in a coiled-up cobra. They have their tea at about midnight, so we should be out by about one-thirty a.m. at the latest. The plasticine for Part One is in Butty's store in the garden, and the rest is on site for Part Two. How did you get on?'

'Splendidly,' Cosie replied. 'Everything is arranged.'

'What a great night it will be! I can hardly wait!' Butty was bristling with excitement. 'It's such a shame no-one will ever know we did it. It's as good as stealing the Crown Jewels.'

They spent the whole of Monday resting. Jess wondered why they did not put in an appearance in the teashop, but concluded that they were perhaps a bit off-colour.

On Tuesday afternoon, their preparations took no time at all. Six of Dr. Webster's knock-out tablets were stuck onto a thick strip of plasticine, and attached to Cosie's collar. Cosie rolled around outside the coalshed until the white parts of his splendidiy-marked coat were darkened down.

Sam left first, and made his way to the Egyptian exhibit. Half an hour later, Butty bellied his way up to Sam, as he had watched his hero Errol Flynn do in countless war films, and was directed to his hiding place. After a further interval, Cosie arrived, and completed the trio of interlopers.

The customers departed at closing time; Gert and Glad came dusted, Glad paying only desultory service to the fear-inspiring cat deities; the Hall was searched, and the security men were locked in. Their associates took up position outside the heavy wooden doors, and everyone settled down for the night.

The inevitable card game got underway, and Cosie was surprised to note that Calder was cheating. While the guards,' attention was thus absorbed, Sam unstuck the plasticine strip from Cosie's collar, and loosened the pills until they would come free at a touch of a claw. Butty emerged from his snake, and bellied his way around to the opposite side of the Hall, using display counters as cover. He was on his way to plant a bomb under Hitler's nose while the High Command sat idly by, ignorant of cat power. He had never been happier in his life.

At last it was midnight. As Sam had correctly guessed, Waterson was a man of clockwork where his tea was concerned. He brewed up and poured three steaming mugs. Just as they sat back for the first sip, they heard tinkling sounds from the far end of the hall. They all put down their tea and rushed over to the apparent source of the noise. As soon as they were clear of the table, Sam and Cosie leapt on a chair and neatly deposited two of Dr. Webster's tablets in each mug, then rushed back to impersonate Anubis again.

Waterson and Calder stood in front of a display of gold-plated chains which were still moving slightly, and which were obviously the source of the tinkling noise.

'I don't understand it. What set that lot moving,' Brown was walking around the display counter on which the chains were set, hanging in line from what was a glorified coat-hangar.

'There must have been a freak draught. It's obvious there is nothing here,' Calder replied, unaware that Butty had already regained the sanctuary of his snake.

'Well, I think it's odd,' Calder said, scratching his head. 'We ought to 'phone Mr. Williams.'

'And a right lot of ninnies we would look. Frightened of shadows! We'd probably never get another job to do. We'll have a look round the Hall, and if everything's all right, we'll just go back and enjoy our tea before it gets cold.' Waterson triumphed, and they lost the chance to foil one of history's great robberies.

The tea had cooled considerably while they were investigating the chains, and they woolfed it down in about three gulps. Sam was relieved to note that Dr. Webster had been correct in describing the American tablets as tasteless. The cats waited in a state of unbearable tension. This was where they would succeed brilliantly or fail ignominiously.

Calder was the first to go. He was in mid-sentence when he slumped forward on the table. Brown stood up, swayed, then sank gracefully to the floor - fortunately not on Mr. Jordan's buttons. Waterson just lolled back in his chair, his head rolling to one side.

Sam, Butty and Cosie remained motionless for ten minutes to make sure all was well. They then went into their well-practiced routine for removing the gems from the tree, and more importantly, getting them out of the store.

Cosie moved across the Hall, stopping in front of a small ventillation grill set six inches above floor level. He hooked his front paws into the grill and pulled gently until it came free, and fell silently onto the carpet. On his last visit, Sam has crawled through the narrow tunnel on the other side of the grill, which fed hot or cold air to the Hall, and undone the clips which kept the cover in place. He had used plasticine to ensure that the grill did not fall out of place in their absence. Cosie retrieved more plasticine from behind the grill, and rejoined Sam and Butty in front of the tree.

'Well lads, this is it. If anything goes wrong, we all rush to the shaft.'

Sam picked his way delicately between Mr. Jordan's buttons. Butty held his breath. He knew he would not have been able to remember where they were, and would probably have triggered the first one. In no time, Sam was on the lower branches, working his way steadily upwards.

The Romanov tiara circled the apex of the tree. It was suspended by two thin threads, and appeared to float freely in the air. Sam securely straddled two branches directly underneath it. He got a good grip with his back legs, and passed his front legs through the tiara, gripping the top point of the tree. Next, he carefully passed his head through, and wiggled his body until the tiara was firmly encircling his middle. He gnawed through the threads, and the tiara was free.

The two necklaces were clasped, each hanging from a branch below and to each side of the tiara. He went first for the emeralds. The necklace was quite long, and he had to wind it twice around his neck. The weight was now considerable for a small cat, and he made his way down to unload. On the way, he picked up a beautiful five-stone yellow diamond ring in his mouth. When he was outside the scope of the buttons, Butty and Cosie unloaded him, and made a glittering, priceless heap of the baubles man had, and would, kill for.

Subsequent trips added the Vanderbilt bracelet, the Romanov sapphires, which almost reduced Butty to tears, a rope of exquisite, creamy pearls, Mrs. Astor's ring, the Empress Josephine's earrings, a ruby ring, set in a shimmer of diamonds, a diamond star-shaped brooch, an emerald ring, and two pairs of diamond earrings.

Butty had the tiara around his middle, and the sapphire necklace wound around his neck. It had a huge diamond pendant, and Cosie had secured this to Butty's collar with plasticine, so his movement would not be impeded. Cosie had the emerald necklace around his neck, and the pearls around his middle. The Vanderbilt bracelet was a tight squeeze around Sam's neck, but it would be only for a short while, and he didn't mind. The brooch was clipped to Sam's collar, and they plasticined the earrings that were left to Cosie's collar. They would each carry a ring in their mouths.

'All ready now,' Cosie said when they were loaded.

'I'll just check we haven't left any clues,' Sam replied, walking over to the Egyptian exhibit. He stuck the strip of plasticine which had held the pills over the huge diamond in the tiara, and looked around for any traces they might have left. There was a small amount of coal dust on the stand, which he blew away, and Butty had left a small clump of gray fur in the cobra. He picked this up, and stuck it on the plasticene covering the diamond.

'That's everything. Let's go!' Sam led the way to the ventillation grill. 'You first Cosie. Keep going until you hit a right turn, then first left.' Cosie crawled into the grill, and was soon out of sight.

'Go on Butty. Just follow Cosie.' Sam turned round to find Butty gazing horror-struck at the grill.

'I'll never get in there Sam. I'm too fat!' Butty's great almond eyes were brimming with tears. 'I've messed everything up. I'm such a stupid, greedy cat!'

Cosie backed out of the grill. 'What's the matter? Why aren't you following me?'

'It's Butty. He's too fat. He can't get himself through the grill.'

The three looked dolefully at each other. To fall at the last hurdle would be unthinkable.

'We'll get you through somehow Butty,' Sam finally said, with more confidence than he felt. 'Cosie, you're the strongest, you will have to push him. I'll back in and pull from the front.'

The tiara was removed from Butty's middle, and placed around Sam. He backed easily into the grill, followed by Butty, who squeezed in with his front paws extended in front of him. It was a very tight fit indeed. Sam grabbed the Romanov necklace that Butty was wearing, firmly between his jaws, and began to inch backwards. Cosie followed Butty, fixed his head firmly against Butty's ample rump, and pushed like a cat possessed. Inch by agonising inch, Butty was dragged through the tunnel, like toothpaste being squeezed out of a tube. At the end of their odyssy, Sam did an amazing somersault which left him facing a grill identical to that in the Jewellery Hall. He quickly sprang the clips, and lowered the grill to the floor. They were, as planned, on a darkened staff staircase which led directly to the Delivery Bay.

Butty was somehow extricated, followed by an exhausted, but triumphant Cosie.

'You wait here,' Sam directed the bedraggled Butty. 'Cosie and I will rush back for the rings and the plasticine.'

They were gone only a matter of moments. They had replaced the grill in the Jewellery Hall, which appeared to have been robbed by wraiths who could walk on alarm buttons, and pass invisibly through locked doors. Cosie neatly placed half the remaining plasticine in strips around the back of the exit grill, and fitted it into place. It was impossible to detect that it had been tampered with.

The world's wealthiest cats passed stealthily down the staircase and into the Delivery Bay. The loosened nails were removed and dropped down a nearby drainhole. they pulled back the plank, and passed into the cold night air. The last piece of plasticine was used to secure the plank in place.

They had done it! They looked triumphantly at each other, and went on their way to stash the loot. It was a cloudy, moonless night, and no glint of treasure could be seen. Just three small shadows going about the lawful business of cats.

At the end of their street, a mere hundred yards or so from The Hey Diddle Diddle, stood an old elm tree. It had been battered by many storms, and provided shelter for many a bird and small animal. Towards the top of the trunk, concealed by thick branches, was a fissure in the bark. It extended quite deeply into the tree itself, and was some six inches wide at the opening. the gnarled branch which concealed it extended conveniently to within easy jumping distance of the high garden wall surrounding the house on the corner.

They took turns to deposit the jewellery in their improvised safe, and finally padded home to await the furore their night's work would generate.

It was two-thirty a.m. when they pushed through the cat-flap and made their way up to the flat. Jess was asleep in a chair. Sam jumped on her lap and touched her cheek gently with his paw. She awoke with a start.

'Where have you been! You've had no supper, and I've been so worried. You must stop disappearing like this for hours. Butty, what on earth has happened to you? You look as though you have been dragged through a hedge backwards.' Not quite, thought Sam, but close.

'Have your supper now, then perhaps we can all get some sleep. Oh, you will all be interested to know that Inspector Radley is a charming host. We went to the theatre, and then went on for supper at Wheeler's. Finally, we went dancing at the Savoy. Do you know, he didn't mention jewel robberies all evening!' Jess was laughing, her good humour perfectly restored. 'Well, now we are all safe at home, I shall leave you to your supper, and go to bed. Goodnight my darling boys.' She kissed them all in turn, and went into her bedroom.

The cats ate ravenously, nervous tension draining out of them with each mouthful.

'There is no point in my going on a diet now,' Butty chortled. 'I am never likely to be in a tight spot like that again!'

Sam and Cosie giggled indulgently. 'You will probably wind up being the fattest cat in the world, and we shall have to pull you around on a trolley.'

Later, as they sat on the rug in front of the dying embers of the fire, they relived the most exciting night of their lives. 'Wasn't it great when I rattled the chains and the guards came rushing over,' Butty considered this to be the high-spot of the night.

'No, I thought it was best when Sam was at the top of the tree wriggling into the tiara.'

'I never realised how strong you are Cosie. Butty is no light weight to push around.'

They carried on excitedly until the reaction hit them, and then fell into a deep sleep in their various favourite spots. They had all agreed that they would give much to be flies on the wall when the doors to the hall were opened that morning.

The robbery was the first item on the BBC News the next day.

'Several items of great value were stolen, although many others were left. the Police are completely baffled as to how the raid was carried out. No alarms were triggered, and the Security Guards on duty outside the doors of the Jewellery Hall neither heard nor saw anything suspicious. The Guards inside the Hall were drugged with a powerful sleeping draught, and are only just regaining full consciousness. Harrods have offered a large reward for the return of the jewels.'

Jess was eating her breakfast, and her cup of tea reached only half-way to her mouth as she listened. The cats were having their morning wash, and Butty looked more or less normal. She was conscious of several sidelong glances from them, and carefully replaced her cup in the saucer to concentrate fully on the news of the robbery.

Butty prowled over and gave her ankles a headbutt, and when they all started rolling about on the floor with squeals of delight, she knew without a shadow of a doubt the perpetrators of what the BBC described as the Great Jewel Robbery.

Jess stared at them incredulously. 'You could not have done it. How could you have carried all those things without your pouches?'

Sam sauntered through to her bedroom, and returned with a necklace wrapped around his neck, and a ring in his mouth.

'Oh Jesus! What on earth are we going to do with it all? Every policeman in the country will be looking for those jewels. Where have you put them? No, it's best I don't know. Radley will undoubtedly be here soon, and I will at least be able to say truthfully that I don't know where they are. If you can pull off that robbery, you can find a safe place to put the jewellery. I'll have to get in touch with Syd immediately.'

Jess suddenly saw the funny side of it, and bust out laughing. Harrods could not have reckoned on such diminutive and ingenious burglars when they perfected their security arrangements. She felt quite sorry for them, and inordinately proud of her gang.

Back at Harrods, the Jewellery Hall was a scene of absolute chaos. Everything was covered in fine, white dust, as the experts searched vainly for fingerprints. Naturally, there were none. The door locks had been tested and found to be in order, as were Mr. Jordan's buttons and bells.

The Assistant Commissioner was head of the investigating team, and was standing near the tree talking to Mr. Jordan.

'What I cannot understand, is why they left so much stuff. There is a king's ransom still on that bloody tree. What do you make of it Jordan? How could they even get near it when there is no room for a foot to land between your buttons?'

'I am as baffled as you, sir,' Jordan responded dolefully. 'Everything is in order, the buttons have not been tampered with in any way. They cannot have been inside when the doors were locked, since six men searched the Hall. It is as if the jewels vanished into thin air. I don't mind admitting that I haven't a clue how it was done.'

Radley was a member of the investigating team, and after about five minutes, felt sure he knew the culprits. When he inspected the Egyptian exhibition, his last remaining doubts evaporated. He even had a notion of how they had got in - although he could not figure out their exit route. Radley walked over to the Assistant Commissioner.

'I don't think there is much I can do here, sir. There are one or two informants I should like to talk to, so with your permission... '

'Yes, I agree. You be on your way. Dangle the reward money in front of them. You never know.'

Radley went straight to The Hey Diddle Diddle, passing directly underneath the cats' safe deposit tree. He greeted Jess, and ordered mince pies and tea.

'Where are they Jess,' he asked as she brought his order.

Jess did not know if he was referring to the cats or the jewels, but thought it wise to assume he meant the cats.

'They are in the back room. Butty is sniffling a bit, and I don't want them catching cold.' She was perfectly composed.

'Been a bit busy lately, have they?'

'Well, you know what Christmas is like. We have been full all the time, and people do love to see them. I enjoyed our outing last night. Thank you once again for a marvellous evening.'

'It was my pleasure. By the way, I don't remember seeing the cats when I picked you up last night.'

'They were all curled up asleep on my bed. As you know, for some strange reason they seem to dislike you, so I put them in my room half an hour before you arrived.'

She lies beautifully, Radley thought. But I know she is lying.

'Have you heard about the robbery at Harrods,' Jess asked guilelessly.

'I am one of the investigating officers.'

'How on earth was it done?'

'I really have no idea, but I don't think we are looking for criminals in the accepted sense of the word. In fact, Jess, I have a very good idea of the team that did it, and even some idea of how they got in.'

He finished his tea with relish, complimented her on her mince pies, and looked pointedly at her. My God, Jess thought, I'm going to blush! He knows, but of course he cannot prove it. He cannot even suggest it without looking a fool.

Radley too was well aware that his chances of catching and charging these particular burglars could be put at minus zero. Give them back, Jess, he wanted to say, then I won't have to hound you.

'The tragedy is that the pieces will be broken up. They are too recognisable to be sold in their present form. the gems will be reset, and be worn by other beautiful women, who will neither know nor care that years of history were destroyed to make their new toys. Fabergé will never again make necklaces and tiaras for the Romanovs. They are totally irreplaceable, as is the ring that Mrs. Astor wore on the Titanic.' Radley sighed, hoping his somewhat romantic approach would sway Jess.

'When will you leave for France?'

'In about a month I think. The Hey Diddle Diddle is sold, and there are only a few loose ends to tie up.'

'I hope to see you before you leave.' He rose wearily to his feet. 'Be careful Jess.'

'What a very strange thing to say Inspector. What on earth do I have to be careful about!'

'Goodbye Jess.'

Late that afternoon, Jess closed the teashop for a short while, walked to the nearest telephone box, and dialled Syd's number.

'I must see you immediately Syd. It's an emergency.

'Can you be at Victoria Station at nine o'clock?'

'Right. Meet you under the clock. Are you all right?'

'Yes. I'll tell you everything when I see you.'

Jess went to great lengths to ensure she was not followed by Radley or anyone else, drawing heavily on Richard's training course. She told Sam, Butty and Cosie to stay at home, and certainly not to go anywhere near the jewellery.

As she waited for Syd, her thoughts went back to 1941, and another meeting - a different station, under a different clock. What if I had known then how things would turn out? Would I still have met Richard, or would I have run as far away as possible? I had my excitement sure enough, but for so brief a time. My ten minutes on the mountain, and how I have longed for him all the time I have been in the valley.

The train from Brighton disgorged its cargo of fractious children, harrassed parents, and other assorted humanity with errands in London. She spotted Syd easily, bustling purposefully towards her.

'Whatever has happened,' he asked, his face drawn with concern.

'Let's go somewhere quiet, and we can talk.'

They went to a Pub in the backstreets of Victoria, where a bored barman was desultorily polishing glasses. There was a secluded booth, and they collected their drinks and settled themselves.

'For Christ's sake, Jess, don't keep me on hot coals. What's happened?'

'It's the Harrods job Syd. The cats did it!'

Syd looked at her in shocked horror. 'Oh my God! Where's the stuff?'

'I've no idea. They have stashed it somewhere safe. The thing is Syd, what in the world are we going to do with it all? Radley has already been to see me. He knows they did it as sure as I am sitting here. It's all going to be very tricky.'

'The only thing he can do is try and pin it on you. He is probably having you watched.'

'He is. A very large and obvious policeman followed me when I left home to meet you. He was easy to lose. Too easy. Radley is smart. There was a woman too, and I almost missed her. Don't worry. I was clean long before I got to Victoria.'

Syd suddenly exploded with mirth. 'I would give a lot to know how it was done. Too bad they can't talk!'

'I've given it a lot of thought too. There was an Egyptian exhibit in the Jewellery Hall, with statues of Egyptian cat deities. I think there may have been three extra deities with very un-Egyptian names on the stand when the store closed. God only knows how they got out with the jewellery. Butty looked as if he had been mangled when they got home, so they must have crawled through something small.'

'I suppose we could do a deal with the insurance people, but it can be risky,' Syd mused.

'Perhaps it sounds silly, but I would feel I had betrayed them. They did a brilliant raid, and they did it for us, so that we could go straight with loads of money in the bank, and no need to worry ever again. I think they also did it to rub Radley's nose in it. They would be so disappointed if we settled for a fraction of what we could get if we took a bit of a risk.'

'You are right Jess. It was their swansong, and we owe it to them to finish the job.'

'One thing does make me sad. Radley pointed out that the jewellery would be broken down into individual stones and reset. It never bothered me before because there was no history attached to the things they stole. This haul is different. There is a wonderful portrait in the Hermitage of Alexandra and the two Archduchesses wearing the Romanov pieces. It was printed in the Express before the exhibition. One of the rings was on Mrs. Astor's finger when she was rescued from the Titanic. It will be a little like murdering a bit of the past to be instrumental in their destruction.'

'I know how you feel.' Syd revered all things old and all things of beauty with roughly equal passion. 'There is one possibility. Remember I told you I made a few contacts with the Americans when they were here? Well, one bloke just might solve our problem. His name is Bud Carlotti, and he told me he had a kind of roving commission for this nutter called Johannes Schmidt. Schmidt is apparently so rich he could virtually pay off Britain's National Debt out of his loose change. He made his money out of diamonds and gold in South Africa years ago. Started off with just a shovel and dug till he hit it big. Then he got fed up with Africa and bought up half of Texas. Naturally, being a lucky sod, he turned out to be sitting on top of a sea of oil. In the last twenty years or so, he's gone a bit loopy, and become something of a recluse. He had a copy of a French chateau built in Colorado, and he never leaves it. He's stuffed it with every work of art he can get his hands on legally - Sotheby's people genuflect at the sound of his name. But what makes him interesting for us is, he pays top prices for stolen stuff too. He could be just what we need. I'll send a telegram to Bud to get here quick, and we'll see if we can do a deal. If Schmidt buys the jewellery, he'll keep it intact. He just loves to possess beautiful things.'

'Syd, what would I do without you? We shall meet often when I am in France?'

Jess, you are my dearest friend, and we'll have the business to run too. Cannes is not the other side of the world. We'll need to meet at least once a month. By the way, I've got all but a thousand pounds of your money to France.' They parted with much affection, and Syd promised he would get a message to her as soon as he heard from Bud.

The following day, Syd sent a telegram to Bud in New York.

'Come Brighton fast. Big, repeat big, item for Schmidt.'

Two days later, Bud walked into Syd's antique shop.

'It had better be big to bring me running this fast, old friend.' Bud was like a ray of sunshine, a huge grin splitting his big, florid face.

Syd closed the shop, and they adjourned to his comfortable house. Over a bottle of Scotch, they caught up on each other's lives since their last meeting at the end of the war.

'I spent a while going round Europe when the Army finished with me,' Bud recalled. 'There was a mountain of stuff lying around, and all at bargain basement prices. I sold everything I owned in the States, and bought everything I could get my hands on. Old Schmidt came up with plenty too. You wouldn't believe the stuff I got for him: paintings, porcelain, silver, jewels. You name it, I bought it. Anyway, I made a fortune, and now I have a real good, straight business in New York. Antiques, just like you. I listened to you, and you made a lot of sense. I am just about as respectable as you can get. Real upstanding citizen. Pay my taxes on time, and support anti-crime campaigns. I owe you a lot Syd. I was just a petty little crook until you pointed me in the right direction. But when you say come fast, I come fast. After all, you can't get too rich can you? What's the deal? Schmidt trusts my judgement completely. I can go sky-high if the loot is worth it.'

'How would he fancy the Romanov tiara, sapphires and emeralds, Mrs. Astor's ring... '

Bud jerked forward. 'The Harrods raid! You're fencing the Harrods raid! Syd you old devil. They are priceless. He'll go over the moon for them.' He gulped his Scotch, and started to gush questions faster than oil from his patron's wells. 'The minute I read about it in New York I wanted to know how it was done. What a fabulous snatch! Who did it, and how? I want to know all about it.'

'I cannot tell you anything Bud. I am dealing with the gang through an old friend of mine. They won't even tell her how they did it. Let's just say it was done by the cleverest cat-burglars in the world, and that the world will not hear from them again. It is their last job.'

Syd would have given much to see Bud's face if he could tell him the identity of the culprits.

'I don't have to tell you how unique the haul is. The papers have listed it all in the great detail. So, will your Mr. Schmidt go to a million pounds for the lot? You add on what you can get, but the price to my cat-burglars is one million pounds clear.'

'He will not be able to resist them. I'm sure he will meet your price. I'll cable him today for confirmation. He likes a bit of drama, and he invented a code we use for these deals. I don't mind indulging the old boy. His confirmation will be here tomorrow. We can sort out the payment details and pick-up arrangements then. You will want the money in Switzerland, of course. There will be no difficulties. So, the business end is tied up. It's so good to see you again, Syd. Tonight we will get stinking lousy drunk, reminisce, and cry for dead friends.'

'There are many to remember Bud. Too many.' One in particular you never met, Syd thought as a bright flash of Richard clutched his heart. Richard in the old shop in Peckham with his first haul; after Dunkirk; with Jess in Brighton. The exhuberant young officer who had changed his life from petty crook to respectable antique dealer, whose bones lay in Germany, and who would never again light a room with his gaiety. Yes, I will get stinking, lousy drunk with you tonight Bud, but you won't know the real reason. I will be getting drunk for Richard.

Syd wrote a letter to Jess telling her to expect a visit from her American 'buddy'. He signed it 'S'. He thought that Radley was unlikely to tamper with His Majesty's Royal Mail, but the letter would not provide any useful pointers if he did. He posted the letter in time for the last collection. Jess would receive it in the morning.

Bud breezed into the genteel atmosphere of The Hey Diddle Diddle with all the restraint of the Fifth Armoured Division crossing the Rhine. Jess saw a tall, well-built man with a florid, round race. His hair was cropped close to his skull, and his clothes marked him as unmistakeably American. She seated him at one of her dainty, round tables, and her small chair gallantly supported his bulk, although he did ooze over the sides of the seat.

'It's a real pleasure to meet you ma'am,' he boomed. 'I heard all about you from my little brother. He says he surely would have died without your nursing in the hospital after D-Day. When I told him I was coming to London, he said I had to be sure to take you out for the best dinner in town.'

Jess admired the way Bud had given her a cover for the benefit of the two policewomen who were delicately sipping tea at the next table, and trying desperately to look as if they had no interest in the conversation.

Sam and Butty strolled over to inspect their American visitor. Butty climbed up onto Bud's lap, and loved him immediately - he had very ample thighs, and a nice line in ear-tickling.

'Great cats you have Jess. Make the place real homey.'

Bud waded through what seemed to Sam a hundred scones and a river of tea, chatting all the time about his mythical brother, his home in New York, and sundry other items of interest.

'So, I'll meet you tonight for the best dinner you ever had, and we'll have a real good time.'

Bud departed, and although there were other customers left, the little teashop seemed empty without his larger-than-life presence.

They did indeed have a wonderful evening, during which Bud confirmed that his Mr. Schmidt would pay them one million pounds for the jewels. The money would be deposited in a numbered account in a certain Swiss Bank. He would hand over the Bank's confirmation letter when Syd gave him the jewellery. He had his own ways of getting them out of Britain and into America, and Jess did not enquire as to his methods. They took a taxi home, and Bud declined Jess,' offer of a nightcap.

'I expect that cop who's been tailing us all evening wants to get home to his bed too,' Bud laughed. 'I doubt he enjoyed himself as much as I did.'

The next day was Sunday. It was a crisp, bright morning, and Jess rose late and lingered over her breakfast. She enjoyed the Sunday papers, which were full of speculation about the robbery and the current whereabouts of the proceeds.

'The difficult part is going to be getting the stuff to Syd. I am sure you have it nearby, but it will be impossible for us to collect it with Radley having the house watched. Sam, you have to show me where it is. We will stage a little pantomime for our friends outside. I'll open the front door, you rush out and I'll chase you. Sit on wherever you have put the jewells, and then I will try to work something out.'

The patient constabulary, who had been sitting in a parked car all night watching the house, were intrigued to see a small, black cat rush out of The Hey Diddle Diddle with what appeared to be a lamb chop in his mouth. He was followed by Jess, shouting 'You bring that back, you bad boy!' The cat ran the length of the street, finally hauling its way up an old tree at the corner. It sat triumphantly on a branch enjoying its chop, while its owner fumed around below. Sam had eaten the meat, and ostentatiously dropped the bone into the crevice in the tree, making much of sticking in his paw.

'All right Sam. I've got it. We can go back now.' Jess made a show of shaking her fist at Sam, and went angrily home.

Jess worried at the problem all day, and it was evening when she arrived at the solution. She told Sam, Butty and Cosie her plan, and they showed their approval with much purring, chin-sucking and headbutting. She then sat down and wrote detailed instructions for Syd, ready to be given to Bud, who was coming to say goodbye in the morning.

Her first visitor that morning was Radley, who dropped in early for tea and toast.

'Has there been any progress?' Jess asked innocently.

'No, but we think the jewellery is still in the country, and we are watching the boys who handle big robberies like hawks. They haven't a chance of fencing it.'

'You look very tired. It must be a hard life being a policeman.'

'Yes it is. Sometimes you have to do things you would rather not do. I just wish whover has the jewellery would contact the insurers. They would be more than happy to do a deal. A Mr. Knight is handling it at Lloyds. Extremely reasonable man.'

When Jess cleared away Radley's breakfast things, she found the extremely reasonable Mr. Knight's business card under the teacup.

Later, after the morning rush, Bud came and made his farewells. Jess gave him Syd's letter wrapped in his bill.

'I'll be on my way then Jess. It's been a real pleasure meeting with you. When you come to New York, you call me, and you'll stay withus. Gina and the kids would just love to have an English lady around the place. You'll be family to us.'

On the Wednesday of that week, the plain-clothes policemen watching The Hey Diddle Diddle paid little attention to a shabby van which parked underneath the tree on the corner. An even shabbier individual emerged, wrapped in an old Army greatcoat, a cap pulled over his eyes, and a muffler round his neck. The figure carried a large saw, which he propped against the tree. He then disappeared into the back of the van, and emerged with a ladder, which he balanced against the tree.

'Better go and see what that's all about,' Constable Fitch remarked to Constable Haynes. Constable Haynes ambled over to where Syd was making a great show of inspecting the tree.

'What's going on here then,' Constable Haynes enquired in the time-honoured phrase of the Metroploitan Police Force.

'Dodgy branches, Guv,' Syd responded from the depths of his muffler. 'Council sent me to saw them off. Can't have them coming down on somebody's bonce.'

'Rather you than me, mate. Can't stand heights myself. Like to keep the old plates firmly on the ground I do.'

Constable Haynes walked back to the car, and settled down again to watch The Hey Diddle Diddle. Radish had some cock-eyed idea that the woman who owned the teashop was mixed up somehow in the robbery, and as usual, it was the minions who pulled the cold duty of watching her. The only things she seemed to be mixed up in were her customers and her cats. You only had to look at her to see she was as straight as they come. sometimes the brass get funny notions.

Syd propped his ladder against the tree. He shouldered his canvas tool bag, picked up his saw, and made his wobbly way up the tree. Jess had sketched the location of the cache, and he had no difficulty in locating it. He pushed his hand inside the cleft in the bark, and felt around. He withdrew his hand, holding a chop bone, and had to suppress the laughter which threatened his balance on his precarious perch. He decided he had better make a show of sawing off a few branches, and attacked one of the larger overhangs. A man in a City overcoat and bowler stopped beneath him.

'From the Council are you? About time they did something about that tree before it brains somebody.' He went on his way, and Syd struggled manfully with another couple of branches.

Now the road was quiet. Only the policemen in their parked car, and a couple of passers-by on the other side. He propped his tool bag against the bark, and unloaded the cats' unusual safe-deposit box. He covered the jewels with an assortment of spanners and screwdrivers, and securely buckled the leather straps.

'Just stretch my legs a bit Jim,' Constable Haynes said to his companion. 'See how that Council bloke is getting on.'

Syd saw him advancing towards the tree when he was still at the head of the ladder. He brushed away a few twigs, hoping the policeman would just pass by. Haynes stopped at the foot of the ladder, and called up.

'All finished then? Here, chuck us your bag while you climb down. You look a bit wobbly.'

Syd felt more than wobbly. His heart was racing faster than ever before, and beads of sweat stood out on his forehead. He had no choice but to bluff it out. He tossed the canvas bag down into the arms of the waiting policeman, praying to gods ancient and modern that the straps would hold. Haynes caught the bag in his big, capable arm, placed it on the passenger seat of Syd's van, and held the ladder while Syd made his unsteady way to the ground. Haynes helped Syd load the few branches he had detached into the back of the van.

'Thanks, mate,' he managed to mutter to the copper who had briefly held in his hands what every policeman in Britain was searching for. He collapsed into the driver's seat, waved a cheery farewell to Haynes, and turned the ignition key. The engine burst into life, then promptly cut out. He was in a panic. He wanted to run. He tried again. Again the engine caught, then died. And again. Syd wished fervently that he had never met Jess. Never heard of Sam, Cosie and Butty, or Harrods, or Romanov diamonds. He wished he was going on his own simple way, making a nice little living, with no 'big farewell jobs'.

Haynes walked round and poked his ruddy face through the driver's window.

'Just got a little mixture problem there, mate. I know a bit about cars. Give us a screwdriver, open up the bonnet, and I'll fix it for you.'

Syd was verging on hysteria. He pulled the canvas tool bag towards him, and fumbled open the straps. Would the tools still be on top, or would the jewellery have worked its way up when he threw the bag to Haynes? There was an assortment of tools on top, and mercifully two screwdrivers. He thrust them at Haynes and opened the bonnet. Haynes fiddled about for what seemeed a lifetime to Syd. Finally, he walked round and told Syd to try it again. The engine fired, coughed a bit, then ran normally.

'There you go!,' Haynes said triumphantly. Only needed a bit of adjustment. It's the colder weather see. You can be on your way now.'

'Thanks a million mate, and happy Christmas. You've been a real help.' Syd pulled away, and had not gone a mile before the reaction set in. He started to laugh wildly, and did not stop until he reached Brighton.

Later, he and Bud stood looking at the loot, set out on Syd's Regency dining table. Bud had thoughtfully provided a fine bottle of vintage champagne, and they toasted each other with delight.

'How will you get them to America?'

'Easy. There is a scruffy old fishing boat taking me to Calais tonight. They are old friends of mine. From there by train to Paris, then onto Schmidt's private aeroplane to Colorado. He is so rich, and has so much clout, his people never, ever get bothered by Customs and Excise.' Bud handed Syd an envelope. 'Here's the receipt from the bank, and the number of the account. That's all the ends tied up, except one thing. I want to drink a toast to our friends, whoever they are. The cat-burglars!'

Syd raised his glass. 'The cat-burglars.'

CHAPTER ELEVEN
A NEW START

Eventually, the Harrods robbery left the front pages, and passed into myth. The police, of course, continued to investigate, watched their various suspects, and kept digging away, hoping for some luck. All except Radley were no nearer to a solution, and as the days went by became thoroughly fed up with the whole thing. Manpower was withdrawn from the case, and Jess lost her shadows. Christmas loomed, and people looked forward to a Happy New Year - as they always had, and always would.

Jess and the cats were spending Christmas with Syd. She would drive down to Brighton, making sure she was not being followed.

On Christmas Eve, she went to Harrods to order one of their superb hampers for delivery that afternoon. She could not resist a visit to the Jewellery Hall, and found it thronged with people. The tree was still splendid with glittering treasure, but Jess noted with amusement that Sam had chosen the cream. Queen Elizabeth's tiara, with the Star of Ceylon sapphire, now had pride of place at the top, and Jess was glad they had not stolen that. The Queen had been such an inspiration in the darkest days of the war.

She stood for a while in front of the Egyptian exhibit. She could see how Sam could blend in, but Cosie was so obviously a tabby, and Butty would have stuck out like a sore thumb. How had they done it? She would never know, and could only marvel at the ingenuity of the brains that had planned it. Sam and Cosie, of course. Butty was a willing workhorse, and adorable, but his thought processes went not a great deal further than his next meal, and the most comfortable place to sleep.

Jess walked home past the strange patchwork left by war. They were still clearing up. Old and beautiful buildings stood side-by-side with devastated ruins. How frail are our dreams, she thought. We think we have our lives worked out, then suddenly we have to start again. Why did you have to die Richard? Why could we not have grown old together?

She found Radley waiting on her doorstep.

'I came to wish you a Happy Christmas Jess,' he said.

'How kind. May I offer you a drink?'

They went upstairs, Radley almost falling over Sam, who was on-guard half way up the staircase. Cosie was out, and Butty was asleep in front of the fire. He awoke as they entered the room, flattened his ears, puffed himself up, and made his peculiar growling noise at Radley.

'Butty bahave yourself,' Jess said sharply, and Butty deflated himself, stopped growling, and sat glowering at Radley with unconcealed hatred.

'Will you be with your family for Christmas,' Jess enquired.

'Yes, my mother likes to have us all at home. I am leaving now for Gloucestershire. And you?'

'I am visiting some old friends in Sussex.'

'Cats as well,' he laughed.

'Of course. I couldn't leave them.'

'And in the New Year you leave for France. I doubt we shall meet again Jess.'

'Oh, you never know. If ever you come to Cannes, you must visit me.'

'I don't think the cats would approve. They genuinely dislike me.'

'Well, I am sure you are popular with other cats,' Jess assured him merrily. 'Mine are a little strange sometimes.'

'I think they are more than a little strange. I think they are quite exceptional. When you go into the antiques business, will they retire?'

'Yes. Their future is a life of sun-filled gardens, pleasure and relaxation,' Jess said hopefully looking at Sam, who sniffed audibly, turned up his nose, and stalked from the room.

'He doesn't seem to approve. I wish you all the luck Jess. I will miss you.'

He took her hand, kissed her gently on the cheek, and took his leave.

'You are a good man, and a clever policeman. I wish you all the luck too.'

Harrods delivered her hamper, and Jess loaded it, her suitcase, and the cats into the car. Sam rode in the front seat, Butty and Cosie in the back. Cosie hated travelling, and was resigned to being sick. Butty made himself comfortable, and planned to sleep all the way. Sam took a lively interest in everything, and sat on top of two fat cushions so he could see out of the windscreen.

They had a wonderful Christmas. Many of Syd's friends came and went, and there was great jollity. Cosie indulged his passion for brown ale, and drank surreptitiously from everybody's glass until he was quite drunk, and collapsed in a heap on Syd's bed. Butty went through his repertoire of tricks, and was fed titbits until he was in grave danger of exploding. Sam followed Jess around, and just enjoyed listening to the good conversation.

On Boxing Day evening they were all alone, and sat relaxing in front of a blazing log fire.

Syd related the saga of the recovery of the jewels, and they all rolled around in great merriment at the unwittingly given assistance of the guardians of law and order.

'So, everything is done. The money is in Switzerland, the jewellery is in America, and that is the end of the Great Jewel Robbery,' Syd concluded, smiling broadly.

'We leave for France in five days. It will all be very strange, but so exciting. A whole new life. In a year's time we will open a wonderful, grand antique shop in London, and we'll never touch anything stolen again.'

Sam thought it all sounded very boring, but if that was what they wanted...

The next few days passed in a rush of packing, ticket buying and farewells.

Finally, they drove onto the Car Ferry for the journey across the Channel. The cats were disgusted to find that regulations required that they travel in a cat-box. Sam and Butty would have enjoyed exploring the ship. Cosie just lay in an agony of seasickness, and prayed for an early death to release him.

Soon, they docked in Calais, and Jess drove them off the ship, and through the bustling port. In a few hours they were driving through the beautiful French countryside. They stopped to picnic and stretch their legs. 'Very much like England,' Cosie said to Sam. 'I think it will be all right.'

Jess was in no hurry, and they motored leisurely through France.

'We arrive in Cannes tomorrow,' she told them one night in the comfort of a rural French Inn. We will rent a house for a month while we look for somewhere to buy.'

The cats fell in love with Cannes immediately. The pretty harbour and broad tree-lined avenues offering the promise of marvellous adventures to come.

'Did you see all those Restaurants with fish in the windows,' Butty exclaimed to Sam and Cosie when they were comfortably ensconced in their rented villa. 'This place is paradise.'

'What about the females? They have a way of walking. I met one in the garden of the house next door. Her name is Zizi, and she is going to teach me to speak French.' Cosie was in love.

'I like the jewellery shops. I sat for ages outside Cartier's yesterday,' Sam sighed dreamily.

Butty and Cosie jumped on him, and Jess found them rolling around in a tangled mass on the lounge floor.

'You all seem to have taken to our new surroundings very happily,' she laughed, extricating Butty and sitting in an armchair with him on her lap. 'I think I have found our home, but I want you to have a look at it before I buy it. After all, you provided the money!'

The house was a delightful Mediterranean-style villa, with a vast unruly garden surrounded by a high wall. There was a rush-fringed pond, inhabited by goldfish whose life expectancy, Jess considered, would be unfortunately short. The Villa had been built at the turn of the century by a rich Parisian as the summer home of his mistress, and its walls could tell many stories if they could but talk. There was a large roof-terrace, from where it was possible to see the sparkling Mediterranean while enjoying a gin and tonic - or a brown ale.

Sam, Butty and Cosie were enthralled. There were trees to climb, bushes to run in and out of, grass to roll about in, and plants to dig up. Everything a cat could want. They demonstrated their approval in the usual manner, and the next day, Jess bought the house, and started on the wonderful task of furnishing it, with more or less unlimited funds at her disposal. She enjoyed herself immensely, and gave full rein to her creative talents. A month went by, then it was ready, and they moved in.

They had a celebration dinner, accompanied by a bottle of champagne for Jess, and some beer for Cosie. Jess had found premises which she would convert into an antique shop, and now their new life was well underway.

When they had been established in Cannes for three months, Syd came to visit them for a week. He thoroughly approved of all Jess had done, and admired her tasteful furnishing of the villa. They had a splendid time visiting all the high-spots of the Riviera.

'Well, Jess,' Syd said one warm evening as they sat sipping their after-dinner coffee and brandy on the terrace of a fine Restaurant overlooking the harbour, 'It's been a long tough haul. There has been prison and poverty and fear and heartbreak. But we made it. Because of our three little friends, we are sitting in the sunshine at last. Bud proposed a toast last December, and I would like to propose it now.'

They raised the big brandy balloons and touched glasses.

'The cat-burglars!'

EPILOGUE

The three years since Jess left England had touched Radley very lightly. He was now Chief Detective Inspector Radley, following his brilliant work on various difficult cases.

One morning he was sitting in his office reading the newspaper, when a particular item made him sit bolt upright in his chair.

'SURPRISE FOR RIVIERA JEWEL THIEVES,' screamed the headline.

'Two men who have been plaguing the French Riviera for months, robbing the homes of Cannes,' wealthy residents, got more than they bargained for when they broke into the home of Miss Jessica Ford, a well-known English antique dealer, two nights ago.

'Apparently the raiders disturbed Miss Ford's three cats, who attacked the villains in a very determined manner.

'At the local hospital, Jean-Luc Castaigne, one of the thieves, related his experience to amazed police officers.

'We were in the library looking for the safe when they came at us. There was a great, fat, gray one who was biting our ankles and scratching our legs, and another big, sleek thing, who got in between our feet and tripped us up. When we were on the floor, this horrible little black one leapt at our faces, and all of them scratched us to pieces. Pierre knocked over a vase, and the crash woke up Miss Ford. She telephoned the police, and that was the end of us.'

'Miss Ford stated that her cats, Sam, Butty and Cosie, had always been especially intelligent and fearless, and that she had rewarded them with a special meal of all their favourite foods.

'A police spokesman said that although dogs had frequently figured in the apprehension of criminals, this was the first occasion where cats had been instrumental in an arrest.'

Radley laughed until tears ran down his cheeks.

'On my side of the fence for once, lads, but you still won!'

If you have enjoyed this novel, perhaps you would like to read one of the other titles published by Malvern Publishing Company Limited

APPLEHURST DISPLAYED by Sarah Coles ISBN 0947993-05-3 £5.95

A delightful book which probes modern village life and exposes the idyll of 'self-sufficiency' for what it really is.

MOUNT SUBASIO by Priscilla Calderini ISBN 0-947993-09-6 £6.95

This is a searching portrait of a little town in Italy, and the experience of a young painter who comes to live there.

IF YOU WAKE AT MIDNIGHT by Daphne Gilfillan ISBN 0-947993-08-8 £6.95

A classic historical romance in which Miss Sarah Rowley, determined to cause trouble to her family, becomes involved with smugglers.

A GENTLEMAN OF QUALITY by Daphne Gilfillan ISBN 0-947993-27-4 £8.95

Daphne Gilfillan's second novel, a delightful romance full of humour and adventure for Hester Radcliffe and her young brother. Very entertaining.

* * * * *

These titles can be obtained from most good bookshops or direct from:

Malvern Publishing Company Limited, P.O. Box 16, Malvern, Worcestershire WR14 1UH.